THE WITCH QUEEN

RITE WORLD 2: RITE OF THE VAMPIRE

JULIANA HAYGERT

COPYRIGHT

 Created with Vellum

RITE WORLD

Welcome to the RITE WORLD!

The Vampire Heir (Book 1)
The Witch Queen (Book 2)
The Immortal Vow (Book 3)
The Warlock Lord (Book 4)
The Wolf Consort (Book 5)
The Crystal Rose (Book 6)
The Wolf Forsaken (Book 7)
The Fae Bound (Book 8)
The Blood Pact (Book 9)

AUTHOR'S NOTE

1

THEA

THE FIRST STEPS AFTER DRAKE LEFT HAD BEEN THE HARDEST. IT took me a long time to take them, and even after ten, twenty, fifty steps, I had to keep convincing myself this was for the best. It sure didn't feel like it. In fact, it felt like I was having my heart and soul ripped from me. Drake had them, and the farther he was from me, the more it hurt.

This was a stupid decision. Why did we have to go our separate ways? We were stronger together. We could find a way to achieve all we had to together; I was sure of it.

Perhaps Drake and I could prepare so when we went back to DuMoir Castle together, we could take out Prince Alex and his allies and start a new, peaceful reign. I would then send word to my coven and let them know I had the heart. Princess Morda would certainly come to pick the heart up in the blink of an eye.

And then ...?

And then, I didn't know. Princess Morda would have a hard time making an alliance with the vampires, even if a good one was in command. She would also never let me stay behind with Drake.

But that was a matter I could worry about later. Right now, all I needed to worry about was going back to Drake and helping him take over DuMoir Castle.

With hope blooming in my chest, I ran back the way I had come. Not even ten yards later, I came to a halt as I realized that Drake, with his super speed, was probably nearing the castle right now. I wouldn't be able to reach him. Not without magic.

Sucking in a sharp breath, I slipped my hand inside the small purse across my shoulders and pulled out the heart. I stared at the red, bloodied mass in my hand. The heart of the first witch in my coven, the Silverblood. The heart had never stopped beating. Even after I took it out of Sarki's chest, the heart kept beating, and for some reason, I thought it beat faster whenever I touched it.

I cradled the heart in my hands, as if it were the most precious thing I owned, and closed my eyes. I should be able to call upon the magic it granted me and send a message to Drake. I would tell him to stop and wait for me. He would be confused, but I was sure he would wait, and once I caught up with him, I would explain my plan to him.

I didn't even have to try to reach for my magic. It simply came to me. Magic from the heart overflowed my veins, rushing through me as fast as blood, filling me with energy and power. I had never felt so powerful. Crap, I had never imagined I could feel this powerful.

Focusing, I sent out my magic, searching for Drake in the vast forest.

A second later, my power faded and fear rushed through me instead.

Slowly, I placed the heart back in the purse and opened my eyes, but I knew I wouldn't see anything. I was surrounded by over a dozen vampires, but they were still hiding amid the trees.

I wrecked my brain, trying to think of what to do. Fight? I wasn't sure I could fight that many vampires by myself. Run? They were too fast for me.

I reached for Drake's dagger inside my pocket. Before I could grab it, the vampires stepped out from their hideouts.

"Well, well, what do we have here?"

"It's Drake's pet."

"How delightful. I think we should play with her."

Trying to cloak my fear with a mask of disdain, I glanced from vampire to vampire. I didn't know their names, but I recognized their faces—they were all Prince Alex's lackeys.

"We were looking for that traitor Drake." One vampire spat on the ground and took three steps toward me. "But Prince Alex told us to kill you if you crossed our path."

I gulped. "I'd like to see you try," I snapped, channeling the bravado I put on so many times while living in DuMoir Castle. On the inside, I was trembling like bamboo in the wind.

The vampires growled and snapped their teeth at me.

What had I done? Provoking them? Was I crazy?

"Our pleasure," one of them said.

They charged me.

Power exploded into me, through me, from me. A bright blue light shone from my hands, and like a wave in the ocean, it rippled out to the forest. It washed over the vampires, killing them instantly and leaving behind nothing but dust.

My heart hammered in my chest as I gaped at the scene, stunned. The heart had been taken from my coven before I was born, making me a weak witch my entire life. Making my entire coven weak, and weaker with each passing year. But I had heard the stories of how powerful it was, of how powerful it could make us, of the tricks a witch could perform when channeling its power. I had even seen some of said tricks, all performed by other covens, and remembered being in awe. And yet, I had never heard of the heart's power being able to decimate a crew of vampires in two seconds flat.

Besides awe, I was now a little scared. I wasn't sure I should be holding such a powerful thing. I hadn't even tried to kill the vampires. What if I tried to do something? To harm someone? I still had to learn how to control and use my powers now that I would have more, but I couldn't imagine controlling the heart.

It was too damn powerful.

But it was probably the only way I could find Drake. I had to warn him Prince Alex's vampires were after him. I had to stop them.

Determined, I reached for the heart once again.

"Thea?"

I glanced up and gasped.

Morda, Princess of the Silverblood coven, appeared from among the trees, followed by Soraya, her second in command, a few witches from her inner circle, and a handful of witchguards. A beautiful witch with long, dark curls and bright hazel eyes, Princess Morda appeared young, in her early thirties, when in fact I knew she was hundreds of years old. Because of our magic, witches lived a long life, but because my coven had lost the heart fifty years ago, the witches were aging faster. It would all be rectified now.

Morda strolled towards me, the hem of her long black

and silver gown brushing the dirty grass—and the vampires' ashes.

"Your highness," I said, bowing my head to her. Despite not being a queen, Princess Morda had been our leader for over a hundred years now.

"Are you well, Thea?" she asked, her tone tight but somewhat concerned. "Soraya warned us there was a commotion inside the DuMoir Castle. We assumed it was you, so we decided to patrol the border of the witch lands, just in case. But then we saw a bright light coming from here."

I opened my mouth to tell her that it had been the heart's doing, but something tightened in my chest. I snapped my mouth closed and swallowed, taking those words down with it. Instead, I said, "It was me, yes. I got the heart and had to fight to get away from the castle. Just now, I was surrounded by vampires, but the heart has given some of my power back and I was able to chase them away."

Morda's brow went up as she stared at me. I hated when she did that. Morda was a powerful witch, and I knew she could break me like a twig with one glance. Her magic was unsurpassed by anyone in our coven since we lost our witch queen a hundred years ago, and as far as I knew, she was a match even for the queens of the other covens.

How she was able to maintain her magic was beyond me, but I was glad someone in our coven had. Otherwise, we would have been crushed by the other covens a long time ago.

"Well done," Morda said, surprising me. She had never praised me before. "For retrieving the heart and getting rid of the vampires."

Soraya stepped forward. With her short silver hair and near-black eyes, she looked cold and hard, and the look of contempt didn't help. "I have to confess, I didn't think you would make it."

Something like fury raced through me. Why did they send me, then? But I knew why. I was one of the weakest, and this was planned as a suicide mission. Even I thought I wouldn't be able to get out of there alive. "I'm surprised too," I confessed.

Morda smiled at me, though it was as hard and cold as Soraya's stare. "Well, we're glad for such a successful outcome. Well done, Thea," she said once more. She swept her hand to the side. "Now, let's go home. We've got a lot to do."

She turned and started marching away. Soraya, the other witches, and the witchguards waited until Morda was in front to follow.

I stayed back, glancing at the trees. My heart broke once again. Somewhere out there was Drake. He was walking into the lion's den alone. I wished I could go to him, send him a message, or kiss him one more time.

However, I had no other choice than to follow Morda home and leave Drake behind.

2

DRAKE

IN THE WOODS OUTSIDE THE DUMOIR CASTLE ESTATE, I GOT ready. I messed up my hair, dirtied my clothes, and for the final touch, I found a sharp rock and swept it across my stomach.

I bit back a scream as the burn spread through my body and blood seeped out.

The gash hurt a lot, but not more than the pain I felt deep inside for having left Thea. I had thought about turning back many times. I wanted to be with her, but I couldn't stroll into the Silverblood coven with her without being killed on sight, and she couldn't come back to DuMoir Castle without being taken as a blood slave by Alex.

Rage tore through me.

Hell, I had always hated Alex, but now I loathed him. I could kill him with my bare hands. But that was too good for him. The bastard had to suffer before I ended him.

There was no choice here. If Thea and I wanted to be together, I had to follow the original plan: I would return to the castle and work to change things from within, while Thea returned the heart to her coven.

Difficult tasks that would take a long time. And the longer I stayed out here, hating everything that was to come, the longer it would take.

I sighed.

With a final prayer to whatever gods Thea believed in, I stumbled back onto the castle's grounds.

As expected, I was found quickly.

"Over here!" a guard shouted as he ran toward me, his spear pointed at my chest.

"Help," I croaked for show. I put a hand on my chest and doubled over, again for show. The slash hurt, but not that much.

Several guards rushed out of the castle and came at me.

"Prince Drake?" Holden, one of my men, stepped from among the crowd and approached me. "What happened?"

"Help," I muttered.

Holden slug my arm across his shoulders and hauled me up. "What happened, my Prince?"

"What do you think you're doing?" Eden asked. He and Ralf approached us with pure hatred in their gazes. They were Alex's men, and I was sure they wanted to kill me right now.

"Helping my Prince," Holden said, loud and firm.

Ralf snickered. "He's a traitor."

"I need to see the princes," I said, my voice low. "I need to talk to them."

"I don't think so," Eden said. "We have orders to capture you, and if you put up a fight, we can kill you."

"He's not putting up a fight," Holden snapped. "He wants

to talk to the princes. I'm sure Alex will want to hear whatever Prince Drake has to say."

Then Lewis, another one of my men, appeared from the crowd. "My Prince." He helped Holden hold me up, then he glared at Eden. "Alex ordered him to be captured. That means Alex wants to see him. Now move before I make you."

Eden growled, but didn't say anything as he stepped aside and let us walk by. The guards closed an arc behind us, pushing us forward, as if making sure Lewis and Holden wouldn't take off with me.

One step into the courtroom and Alex was in my face. "You ... traitor!" he shouted. His brown hair was a mess over his shoulders and face, and his tanned skin turning red with rage. "I will kill you for what you did." He turned around. "Prepare the guillotine."

The princes and vampires inside the courtroom didn't move. They stared. At Alex and me. And I took my time trying to familiarize myself with what had changed since I had been gone.

The courtroom had been cleaned up. The guillotine had been fixed, the injured vampires had been taken to the infirmary —I assumed—and the blood had been wiped from the floors.

"Didn't you hear me?" Alex asked, his voice rising. "Prepare the damn guillotine and let's finish what we started."

Prince Cain ignored Alex and walked to me. "Why did you come back?"

"Why would I not?" I glanced at the guillotine on top of the wood platform. "I don't understand. Traitor? Execution? What's happening?"

Cain's eyes widened. "What do you mean? You don't remember?"

"I ... I don't know. Just now I found myself in the woods, fighting a witch. She injured me." I gestured to the bloody gash on my stomach. "But I have no idea how or why I got there."

Alex scoffed. "Are ... are you saying you can't remember anything?"

"Anything what?" I asked, feigning innocence.

"Lord Reynard! Prince Albert! You killed them both," he shouted. "And a couple of hours ago, we found Sarki's body. It seems your witch did kill her."

I put on a mask of shock and pain. "L-lord Reynard is dead? Prince Albert and Sarki too?" I shook my head. "No, no, that can't be." I blinked. "I remember ... I remember the ball. I saw them all at the ball. I talked to Sarki at the ball. And then ..." I blinked again for effect. "And then I don't know. The next thing I remember is fighting the witch in the woods and running back here."

Prince Gray stepped forward. "She must have put a spell on you."

"Who?" I asked.

"The witch," Dorian said. "Thea. Don't you remember her?"

I frowned, as if I were reaching into the depths of my mind and coming up blank. "No ... was that the witch I fought in the woods?"

"Apparently," Cain said.

"You're all buying this?" Alex asked, looking at each prince. "That the witch spelled him?"

"It sounds plausible," Phelps said. "She was powerful enough to kill Sarki and fight us all. She could have easily put a spell on him."

"No, that's absurd," Alex retorted. "Drake was planning

something with the witch. He killed Lord Reynard and Prince Albert, and she killed Sarki. They were in this together."

"That doesn't make any sense, Alex," Gray said. "Why would Drake ally with witches? We all hate them. Besides, Drake doesn't remember anything from the ball on. That was when she approached him. That must be when she started the spell."

Alex growled. "Now you're going to tell me you believe Sarki killed Lord Reynard and Prince Albert."

"The witch used blood magic to show us her memories," Patrick said. "That can't be changed."

"All lies!" Alex's face became even redder. "It was another trick, another spell. She pretended to be using blood magic. And now our dear Prince Drake comes back conveniently not remembering anything. Don't you see how all the pieces fit too well? All lies!"

"Alex, calm down," Prince Nolan said. "Let's say you're right and Drake is lying. We still need to investigate this before executing him. You don't want your first act in the castle to be unjust."

First act in the castle? What the hell did that mean?

"I'm not lying," I insisted, despite the red flags going on all around me. "Hell, I can't believe Lord Reynard, Prince Albert, and Sarki are gone. That's ... that's not true."

Lewis clutched my shoulder. "I'm sorry, my Prince. I know how much Lord Reynard meant to you."

"Stop with this nonsense!" Alex shouted. He was all about shouting tonight. "Put him back in the guillotine and let's end this shit right now!"

"Alex, please," Dorian said. "Nolan is right. You don't want to start your reign by condemning a dear prince to death." I barely contained the gasp that wanted to rip out of my chest. "Let's investigate this and be smart about it."

Alex glared from him to me and back to him.

His first act. Reign. Then, I saw it. Lord Reynard's silver cross pendant with the thin chain hanging from Alex's neck. Somehow, Alex had become Lord of the castle in the last twenty-four hours.

A heavy ball of dread and disgust sank into my stomach. It seemed my mission in this castle had just gotten a whole lot harder.

Alex let out a long breath. "All right. We'll investigate this, but I have two demands. One, Drake will continue being a prince in name only with no real power, he has no voting rights and no voice among the princes anymore. Two, Drake will be executed immediately if he's lying. The other vampires need to learn what happens if they lie to me, too."

Eden and Ralf entered the room then, carrying Thomas with them.

"My Prince," Thomas said, looking at me with wide eyes. "What's happening?" His gaze found the cut across my stomach. "Are you okay?"

I glared at Alex. "What are you doing?"

"Someone has to pay," he said.

"For what? I wasn't myself. Even if I committed crimes, it wasn't me. I was out of my mind and forced to do things I didn't want to. Thomas has nothing to do with it."

"I don't care," Alex said. He nodded to Eden and Ralf. "I need to set an example."

Eden and Ralf pulled Thomas to the center of the room— toward the guillotine.

"Alex," I called out. I pushed Lewis and Holden away and

approached Alex. "Please, Alex, he's a boy. He can't be punished for my crimes."

Alex leaned over me. "Don't you see you're the one being punished here?" He then turned and approached the guillotine.

"No," I said, stumbling closer. The other princes closed in around me. "Please, Gray, Phelps, Cain ... help me here. He can't do this."

Phelps sighed. "He's the Lord of the castle now. He can do pretty much anything."

"We already stopped him from killing you," Cain said. "That's all we'll get from him right now."

Despair flooded my senses. No, this couldn't be it. There had to be a way. Alex couldn't be this cruel. Except, he was. I knew he was. He had been the cruelest prince I ever met in my five hundred years. He killed humans for pleasure every opportunity he had. Of course he would kill Thomas, a human I cared about, because it angered me and that pleased him immensely.

"Prince Drake!" Thomas cried as he was pushed down the guillotine and strapped to the sides. "My Prince!" A sob broke his voice. "Please, save me."

I pushed through the burn of my injury and charged to the platform. A hand closed around my arm before I made it two steps out.

"Don't be stupid," Cain hissed. "If you interfere in any way, you're next. And there will be nothing we can do to stop Alex then."

He was right. I knew he was right, but it was Thomas. I couldn't let Thomas die. He had suffered too much in this life already, and it had been because of me. I couldn't be the reason his life ended, so short and unhappy.

Ignoring Cain's words, I pushed through. Only to have too more hands hold me back.

"If you won't listen to reason, then we'll make you," Gray said.

"Close your eyes," Phelps warned.

But I didn't. I couldn't.

I listened as Thomas's cries echoed through the room. I watched as the blade came down and his cries stopped. My stomach revolved, and my legs gave out when his head fell on the stone ground with a dull thud.

Lewis and Holden appeared by my side and held me up. "We'll take you to the infirmary now."

I protested, or at least I thought I did. I opened my mouth to yell, but no sound came out. I jerked against Lewis and Holden, but I was too weak from the blood loss and too shaken to really do anything. They carried me out of the room as the other vampires advanced on Thomas's fallen body to drink the remaining blood.

3

A PANG CUT THROUGH MY CHEST AS THE VIEW CHANGED FROM the dark, closed forest, to a deep valley and the expansive estate below. The fields extended for miles, and right in the middle sat a sprawling mansion. The enchanted gray stones of the façade were marked by panels of three tall, but narrow windows side-by-side, every ten feet. The tops of the windows were arched, climbing into tiny peaks, before sweeping down. Balconies extended from the stone beneath each set of windows. Potted plants hung from the rails, dangling fuchsias, clematis and ivy. Their fragrance encompassed the estate, even this far from the mansion.

The Silverblood Estate was the house of all our coven witches.

My home.

We crossed the invisible magical barrier that protected us from unwelcomed visitors, and went down the winding path until we reached the main gate. Morda waved her hand and the tall, iron gates opened—only a handful of witches could open the enchanted gate like that. I was certainly not one of them.

A servant, dressed in plain white pants and a shirt, waited for us at the entrance. He bowed as Morda walked past him. She didn't acknowledge him. The same happened with the next three servants we crossed—two males and one female. All humans.

Now, after seeing the blood slaves at DuMoir Castle, I wasn't sure our servants weren't slaves after all. They dressed a little better, they had fuller meals, they had a hidden house carved into the side of the hills behind the mansion, and though they weren't kept behind bars unless they misbehaved or betrayed us, they were still locked away here, forbidden to leave. They had lost their freedom, and I was pretty sure that made them slaves.

Especially the males.

Men were treated like toys in our society. The pretty ones were forced to dress inappropriately, without shirts, wearing tight pants or shorts, or wearing nothing at all, and they were used for sex whenever a witch felt like it.

I shuddered at the thought.

The doors to the great hall opened, and I took a sharp breath. Imposing and regal, this place never ceased to take my breath away.

It was wide and long, with shiny gray stone floors that reflected our images, and a curved cathedral ceiling, burdened with heavy crystal chandeliers. Mirrors covered the thick archways, and at the end of the room, three steps led to a raised platform where a throne stood. The chair was supposed to be occupied by our witch queen, but it had been Morda's for over a hundred years now.

A handful of witches were already there, at the base of

the steps, waiting for us—Adya, Polina, Vera, Liliana, and the rest of the princess's inner circle. They all bowed to Morda as she approached them.

"Liliana, dear," Morda said, reaching for one of them. "You don't need to bow in your state." Liliana placed her hands in Morda's and stood straight.

My eyes widened as I took in her round belly, and I understood why Morda was being so sweet to her. Liliana was pregnant! I didn't remember her being pregnant when I left. Maybe she hadn't known it yet? But it had been a couple of weeks. Perhaps I hadn't paid attention to that before.

It was rare for witches to get pregnant. Many tried for years before conceiving, and even then, nothing was certain. Witch pregnancies were difficult and painful, and most of them ended naturally before the six-month mark. By the looks of it, Liliana was further along. A plain miracle.

"I'm fine, your highness," Liliana said, smiling. "I think the baby will make it this time."

If it was a girl …

I winced with such thought. Even if a witch made it to the end of the pregnancy and had the baby, it was all for nothing if the baby was a boy. Boys were killed at birth since no man was allowed to carry magic in our society. I had heard of only one baby boy who had been hidden away by his mother and reached adulthood many years before I was born. A warlock. That was what witches called him. The warlock was found and killed anyway.

I confess I had never stopped to think how barbaric and cruel our society was. It was only after spending time with the vampires and seeing their cruelties toward humans, toward me, that I understood. That I felt such pain.

It disgusted me.

Morda placed her hand on Liliana's belly. "By all that is sacred, let's hope so."

Liliana grinned in delight. I knew how she felt. It wasn't easy to be praised by Morda—and she and I had received such attention today. I bet Liliana was one of Morda's priorities now, while I would be forgotten once I handed the heart to Morda.

As if they could read my thoughts, two witchguards, dressed in their thick black and silver armor, came into the room through one of the side doors, carrying a big polished box by its silver handles. With a bow, they deposited the box in front of Morda, then opened the lid.

Morda turned to me. "Please, Thea, bring out the heart."

For some reason, my hands shook as I reached inside my purse and pulled out the heart. As it had before, the heart's beating grew faster in my hands, and I felt its power brushing against me.

With a huge smile, Morda took the heart from me, cradling it like a precious newborn, and lifted it high. "Our coven's heart is back!" she cried.

The witches in the room shouted in response, unaware of the shock that came when the heart was snatched from me. *Stolen.* That was how it felt.

"What a feat, Thea," Soraya said, her cool eyes drawing goose bumps from my arms. "Congratulations in successfully completing your mission."

"It was my duty," I said, an automatic answer that left a sour taste to my mouth. Until a few weeks ago, I would have laid my life down for this coven without hesitation. Now? Now I was questioning every single thing they did or said.

While the other witches congratulated me, Morda stared at the heart with hungry eyes. We all knew she had tried being the queen of our coven many, many times, before the heart was stolen, but it still rejected her now.

Morda deposited it in the red velvet lining of the box, then closed it. She beckoned for the same two witchguards to take the box away, probably to return it to the sanctuary, a sacred place at the top of the tower on the west side of the mansion. After another bow to our princess, the two witchguards scurried out of the room, taking the heart with them.

A heavy ball expanded in my chest.

I felt like they were taking my own heart away.

"We have the heart back now," Morda started, and the witches calmed down. "But not all is well yet." She looked at me. "Blackmarsh, Bluemoon, and the other covens are getting bolder. They've been on the move, and since the rumors that Lord Reynard fell within his own castle have spread, there has been unrest." A wicked grin appeared on her red lips. "Tell me, Thea, is Lord Reynard really dead, or is that a rumor the vampires are spreading as a trap to get us?"

I gulped. "It's true. He was killed my first night in the castle."

"Fabulous. Who killed him?"

"The oracle."

"Sarki?" Morda's brow slammed down. "But I had always heard she was devoted to him."

"It was a facade. She hated the man."

"And where's she now?"

"Dead."

Morda's eyes widened. "What happened?"

"She was hiding our coven's heart, not Lord Reynard. So I killed her."

The smile that spread over her entire face sent a chill down my spine.

But it was Soraya who spoke next. "You killed the oracle? And to think you were one of our weakest. Well done, Thea. Really well done."

"As I was saying." Morda took back the spotlight. "The other covens are on the move and they have witch queens." An invisible weight fell over all of us. It was an embarrassment to not have a queen. "If we want to win ... By all that is sacred, if we want to survive what's coming, we need a witch queen."

Whispers started. I guess everyone was wondering the same as me. How would we find a witch queen? Although the heart gave strength and magic to the entire coven, it contained power that was only granted to one who was worthy, to a witch it chose to yield its special magic. And so far, the heart hadn't chosen a conduit in over a hundred years. A coven would lose its magic without a heart, but without a witch queen? A coven wouldn't survive forever without a queen, as the queen was its ultimate protector. And since the other covens were aware of our situation—heartless and queen-less—they had finally started to move on us. We had the heart back now, but unless Morda found a coven member who could be the witch queen, I had no idea how she would solve this problem.

"We can all agree with that," Soraya said. "But how do you intend to find our queen?"

"We will produce one," Morda announced with a smile. "In order to save the coven, one of us must produce the queen. Every witch in the coven must become pregnant to heighten the chances of producing an offspring the heart will accept as queen."

I gasped as the reality of the situation fell over me. Get

pregnant? To get pregnant, one had to have sex. A woman needed a man.

I needed Drake.

"That sounds a little drastic," I dared to say. All eyes fell on me, but none of them shot me with invisible fireballs like Morda.

"Drastic times call for drastic measures," Morda said, her voice devoid of emotion. "This is not open to negotiation. All witches of this coven, regardless of their rank, will try to produce an heir starting immediately." She turned to Liliana with a fake smile. "Not you, dear. You've already succeeded." Then, she beckoned toward the doors behind us. "Go now. All of you. Go to your rooms and do your duty to the coven."

Six witchguards stepped forward and closed in on us, ushering us out without having to lay a finger on us.

My hands trembled as I followed them like an obedient little witch. The witchguards took us up the main staircase and into the hallway leading to our bedrooms. Like a convoy, we stopped only long enough to allow a witch inside her bedroom before moving on to the next door.

My bedroom was next, and I was relieved I could hide in there. I had no idea how and when Morda wanted us to get pregnant. Was she planning some sort of party with the men, so the witches could easily take them to bed? If that were the case, then I had to come up with an excuse as to why I couldn't go. Like, I was so exhausted after my mission or I was sick.

Morda wouldn't buy that lame excuse.

Regardless, once I was inside my bedroom, I could relax for a few minutes before having to worry about a plan—how was I going to not sleep with a stranger.

The witchguards paused in front of my door.

Without acknowledging them, I pushed my door open and hurried inside. I locked the door and leaned against it, letting out a long, relieved sigh.

"Lady Thea?"

I stared at the man in front of me—a man wearing what seemed like a loincloth that only covered his male bits, leaving his entire torso bare.

I gaped. "Who are you?"

4

DRAKE

THE HEALER DIPPED A COTTON BALL IN A BOWL WITH A GREEN paste.

"This is gonna hurt," she said.

I braced myself, but the burn that came when she spread that green paste and its foul smell over my wound was much stronger than I had anticipated. I groaned and jerked, cursing the devil and all his offspring. I was sure I would have given in to the pain—and everything else taking over my mind, my soul—and I would have lunged at the poor healer, squeezing the life out of her body, if Lewis and Holden hadn't held me and pressed me back against my bed.

My bed, where Thea and I had made love for the first time.

My bed, in my chambers, where Thomas was supposed to be safe.

"Get out!" I barked.

Trembling, the healer gathered her stuff and ran.

"Calm down, my Prince," Holden said, still pushing me down. "You'll scare the entire castle away like this."

"Good," was my reply. Let them go. Then, I wouldn't have to come up with a plan to take over the castle. It would be mine by default.

"Prince Drake, please, try to relax or—"

"Relax!" I cut Lewis off and finally broke free of their hold. I sat up in my bed and snarled at them. "They just killed Thomas for no good reason, and I'm supposed to relax?"

"If you don't, Lord Alex will be more suspicious than he already is," Holden said.

Lord Alex. I hated hearing that title in front of his name. He didn't deserve it.

I forced my face to relax and pinched my brows together, as if I were confused. "Suspicious of what?"

"Of your memory loss," Holden said in a low voice.

"You don't believe me?"

Holden and Lewis exchanged a glanced. Then Lewis cleared his throat. "We're definitely not judging, my Prince, but it does seem rather convenient that the witch had you under her control."

I pressed my mouth together. Holden and Lewis had been my men for centuries now, and I knew I could trust them, but for some reason, I didn't want to tell them. Not yet. Not until it was the right time.

"It's the truth," I snapped, already tired of the lies. "That bitch seemed to have fun though with all I supposedly did while she controlled me." A sour taste filled my mouth after calling Thea a bitch. She was the furthest from being that, but I had to keep up appearances. I grabbed a towel from the nightstand and started wiping the damn green paste from my chest. "Now, if you're not here to tell me it was all a dream, and Thomas is raiding the kitchen again, then I suggest you leave."

The two vampires exchanged a look again. That was seriously annoying me.

"As you wish, my Prince," Lewis said, bowing.

"Call us if you need anything." Holden dipped his head.

I watched as the two marched out of my room and closed the doors behind them. I remained still, listening to their retreating footsteps. After a moment, they crossed the front doors to my chambers. They greeted the six guards Alex had stationed outside my door—curiously, none of them were my men—before leaving.

I lay down in bed and closed my eyes.

Shit.

Shit, shit.

If I had known Thomas would be killed, I wouldn't have come back. I was sure it was only a matter of time before Alex charged in here, found the boy, and tortured him for information before killing him.

That didn't make it easier to swallow.

Hell, Thomas was gone. Thea was far away. Alex had been proclaimed Lord of the castle. And I was alone, swimming with the sharks and deprived of my title. I was like any other slave; I just didn't wear rags or sleep in the slave quarters.

Shit.

I had no time to waste. I wouldn't let Thomas's death and my separation from Thea be a waste. I would avenge him, and I would do it fast because I wasn't sure how long I could take Alex parading around like a king inside this damn castle, committing cruelties like a human changes shirts.

To be honest, I also wasn't sure how long I could stay away from Thea.

Groaning, I reached for one of the four bottles of blood on the nightstand. I felt weak and disoriented and lost. I would drink blood until I felt stronger and stopped pitying myself.

I needed to act.

I drained the first bottle in three seconds, then reached for the second one.

Soft footsteps echoed inside my chambers. I sat up again and listened. The steps belonged to a woman, for sure, and they were coming my way.

Gritting my teeth, I got up from bed, picked up a shirt from one of the armchairs, pushed my arms through the sleeves, and had enough time to ready for a fight before the door opened.

"Who are you?" I barked.

The young woman stared at me with her hazel eyes. "My Prince." She bowed her head. "My name is Luana."

Her cheeks had an unusual golden tint, her long light brown hair had a messy wave, and her heart beat fast. She was human.

"What are you doing here?"

"I was sent to be your new blood slave."

What the hell? What game was Alex playing? First, he complained that I was a human lover, that I had taken too many blood slaves over the years, and now he was offering one to me? This didn't feel right.

I scoffed. "Did Alex send you? To spy on me, I'm sure. Well, tell him I'm grateful for the offer, but I'm not interested."

"Prince Drake, I—"

"I said I'm not interested. Just go."

The young woman put both her hands on her waist and glared at me. "Believe me, if I could, I would leave right this instant. I don't want to be here, but if I leave, Lord Alex will kill me."

Shit. "And I'm supposed to care why?" I suppressed a wince at my words. Of course I cared. I had always cared when humans were killed without cause.

"Because ... because I heard you're a good prince and you help your blood slaves."

Was she kidding me? "Haven't you heard my blood slave was killed by Alex a couple of hours ago?"

Her heart sped up and she swallowed. Her scent filled the room, and I wrinkled my nose—her smell seemed tainted. She probably had some kind of poison in her veins. The moment I bit her, which was what Alex wanted, I would fall immobile. Then Alex would come in and finish the job.

"I have," she whispered. "But he lasted a long time with you. If I leave now, I'll be killed on the spot." She paused and her eyes hardened. "I don't want to die."

Hell ...

I couldn't take another one under my wing. I couldn't. They all died anyway. If they weren't killed by other vampires, they eventually grew old and died. What did it matter if it was today or tomorrow? Or in ten years?

I pressed my eyes shut and berated myself. What the hell was I thinking? I was being cruel and uncaring because I was hurting.

I didn't want this girl here, but shooing her away wasn't the answer.

"Stay here tonight," I said. "Just pick a bedroom and sleep

there. And be quiet." I waved her off. "We'll talk about this tomorrow."

"Thank you, my Prince." She dipped her head once more, and like a quiet mouse, she scurried out of my bedroom, closing the door behind her.

I ran a hand over my face. What the hell had just happened?

This was too much.

I grabbed another bottle of blood and stepped out onto the balcony. I leaned over the stone rail and looked up at the full moon and the many clouds surrounding it. This same moon shone over Thea wherever she was. She should be back at her coven right now, somewhere inside the Silverblood estate.

Hell, I shouldn't have come back. I should have followed Thea. No, I should have convinced her to send the heart back to her coven and run away with me. I should have let her convince me of that.

Screw the princes and the other vampires and my entire coven. It was stupid trying to be noble. Now, the mess in this castle was even bigger, and I had no idea how to fix it.

I lifted the bottle and gulped the blood in seconds. After having drunk from Thea, these bottles of blood felt plain, tasteless. But it was all I had, and I would need my strength if I were to start a rebellion from inside the castle.

I looked at my chest. The slash was almost closed, a sign that I was recovering and the blood was effective. Soon, I would have only a red line, and later smooth skin.

I glanced out to the maze in the back garden and let my mind roam free along with my eyes.

Movement crossed my peripheral sight and I sharpened my focus. A large, shadowy shape ran on all fours.

It couldn't be.

I leaned over the rail to get a better look as guards appeared outside the garden.

"We have an intruder!" Alex cried out, barging out from inside the castle.

I still felt weak and dizzy, but I used my super strength. In three jumps, using archways and windowsills and columns, I was out in the garden with them.

The other princes rushed out of the castle, all ready for battle.

"Where is it?" Cain asked.

"What is it?" Dorian cried.

"It's a werewolf," I said.

Alex turned around and narrowed his eyes at me. "Since you're here, this will be on you."

I blinked at him. "What?"

He crossed his arms with a triumphant grin. "Prove yourself trustworthy again. Hunt the werewolf and bring it down."

"We should go," Patrick said. "It's getting away."

"No," Alex said. Was I the only one who could hear the challenge in his tone? "Drake will go. Alone. And he'll bring its dead body to us."

I gritted my teeth. "And if I don't?"

He grinned at me. "Then you're next."

5

My bedroom still looked the same: an open area with a loveseat and a side table holding a stack of books I was reading before I left. Behind the sitting area, my comfy queen bed and its dark blue comforter and my four fluffy pillows. Two nightstands flanked the bed, also covered by books. To the right, two doors: my closet and my bathroom.

However, the man in a skimpy leather skirt standing between the love seat and the bed was a new addition.

"Who are you?" I repeated the question.

The man lowered his gaze. "My name is Keeran, my lady."

"What are you doing here?"

"I was sent by Princess Morda, my lady."

I gritted my teeth. "Of course."

Not only had she ordered us to procreate, Morda ensured we wouldn't waste time by sending servants to our bedrooms beforehand.

I opened my mouth to send him away, but realized I couldn't. If Morda found out I sent Keeran away without even touching him, she would punish me and kill him without hesitation.

The man shifted his weight, drawing my attention to him. I couldn't deny he was handsome with his dark brown hair cut short, which enhanced the sharp lines of his face. His tall figure, wide shoulders, and hard muscles helped too.

He was hot, sure, but my heart was with Drake. My stomach curled for even imagining myself touching this man.

My stomach tightened more for finally making out the many marks on his chest, stomach, arms, and shoulders. They were scars. And apparently, some had been recent as there was still dried blood caked on them.

I took a step toward him.

He matched my stride and retreated a step. "You'll have to use magic to force me to have sex with you," he said, finally lifting his eyes to meet mine. They were a warm shade of brown. "You're gonna have to rape me, like the other witches do."

Could I get any sicker this evening? This was ridiculous.

I raised my hands, palms facing him. "Relax, Keeran. I have no intention of having sex with you."

His thick brows slammed down. "But ... Princess Morda said—"

"Never mind what she said." I gestured to the love seat. "Now, sit down and we'll take a look at your wounds."

His eyes widened. "W-what?"

Shaking my head, I walked past him and went to my bathroom. I found the herbs in my vanity and mixed them using the mortar and pestle I kept beside the sink. There was one strong and rare herb I didn't have here, valerian, but I wouldn't dare going out to get it now. The salve wouldn't be as potent, but it would still be much better than leaving all those wounds open and prone to infection.

When I returned, Keeran stood in the same spot, his eyes wide and his stance wary. How could I explain to him that I wouldn't rape him, that I wouldn't even touch him like that, in a way he would believe me?

I placed a jar with clean water and a rag on the side table, and I sat down on the love seat, the mortar and pestle on my lap. "Keeran, by all that is sacred, I won't hurt you, and I won't force you to do anything you don't want to. I just want to clean your wounds and apply something to them before they all become permanent marks on your skin." I patted the spot beside me.

Like a rabbit watching a fox, Keeran moved, his steps slow and measured. I practiced my patience while waiting. If I complained or said something, it would only take longer.

Finally, he sat down beside me, but he kept his gaze down. "Some have been there for years. I'm sure they are all permanent."

"We'll see about that." I wetted the rag and started cleaning the recent wounds. They were all over his shoulders and shoulder blades. "What happened?" He glanced at me, then lowered his gaze again. It hit me that he was young, younger than I first thought. He was probably twenty-one or twenty-two—just a year or two older than I was. And he had suffered so much already. "I hope you realize quickly that I'm not like the other witches, or our situation here will only be harder. For instance, you can look me in the eyes and you can talk freely. I'm not going to punish you for anything you do. Unless you try to kill me. Then, I'll be forced to defend myself."

He swallowed then brought his eyes to mine. This man

was easily twice my size, and yet he looked at me with terror in his eyes. I couldn't imagine what the other witches had done to him to make him this terrified.

"I was whipped for resisting Lady Soraya," he confessed, his voice low.

I pressed my lips together. "She tried to sleep with you?"

"She raped me, before and after whipping me."

I stilled, unsure what I felt the most—shock or disgust. "I'm sorry." I dropped the rag and mixed the herbs one more time. "This might sting a little, but I promise it'll clean any impurities and help them heal faster."

Keeran hissed and his muscles contracted when the healing paste touched his first wound. I braced myself for a second, sure he would curse or complain, but after that, he took it all like a champ.

"Why are you doing this?"

"What?" I asked as I spread the salve on the last wound right in the middle of his shoulder blades. "Not forcing you to sleep with me, or cleaning up your wounds?"

"Both."

I finished and set the mortar near the books on the side table. Then, I sighed. "Let's say I changed."

Though I had never raped a servant before, I had slept with a couple here and there. It was normal to the witches; it was part of our society, of our upbringing. It had been normal to me. Until I met Drake.

"I heard you came back from a secret mission, one that was supposed to be hard," he said. "Actually, I heard rumors of it being a suicide mission. Was that what changed you?"

I reined in a grin before I scared him—he was still wary of witches, after all. "Yes, that's right. It was a suicide mission and somehow I made it. And this mission changed me."

"How?" He winced and looked down at his feet. "Sorry, my lady. I shouldn't have asked that."

"I said you can talk freely. That includes questions. I also said you can look me in the eyes when talking to me." I paused. "And I'm adding a third rule: Don't call me my lady. I'm Thea. Call me Thea."

"I can't ..."

"Yes, you can. At least when you're inside these walls, you can."

Keeran returned his eyes to mine. "I feel like I'm dreaming. I have never come across a kind witch, and I've lived here for years."

I frowned, wondering how I hadn't met Keeran before. Actually, I probably didn't know the majority of servants in this mansion. I had never cared for them or their fates before.

And now I did.

I stared at Keeran, wondering if he wanted in on the plan brewing in my head. It was risky. If I shared my plans with him and he betrayed me, if he went running to Morda to tell her everything, I was done for. And yet, the shock in his gaze when I was kind to him, when I offered to clean his wound ... he hadn't faked it, I was sure.

"I was always a weak witch, one of the weakest in the coven. I was picked on by more powerful witches, teased. I hated it. I hated being me," I confessed. "So when Morda said she had a dangerous mission, I volunteered because I wanted to prove to them that my magic was weak, but my soul, my heart were not. I wanted to show them I belonged to this coven as much as they did. That I had a place here and could do more than they thought. To my surprise, I was chosen." I still couldn't believe I had made it. "Everyone knows we haven't had a witch queen in over a hundred years, but what rumors have you heard about the coven's heart?"

"I ..." He looked lost, as if he wasn't sure he should tell me.

I went to touch his hand, to reassure him I was on his side, but I remembered he had been touched without permission thousands of times. I folded my hands in my lap again. "It's okay, Keeran. I won't punish you, I promise."

"Hm." He cleared his throat. "The two servants favored by Morda like to talk, but I found out most of what they say are lies, and they said the heart had been stolen a long time ago and the witches were weakening."

I nodded. "That's not a rumor; that's true."

I told him about my mission. I told him I had been sent to Castle DuMoir, the headquarters of the most powerful vampire coven on this side of the globe. I told him I was supposed to be placed with the other slaves, but ended up as a personal blood slave to Prince Drake, who in the end proved to be more than an arrogant prince. I told him the lord of the castle and a prince were murdered and that Drake was a suspect. I told him someone had tried to kill Drake, but I saved him, revealing what I really was. And that Drake didn't run away or turn me in or kill me. I told him Drake decided to help me. However, Drake had been caught, framed for the murders, and I was left alone to find the heart. I told him I found the heart—inside the oracle's chest—retrieved it, and saved Drake from execution. I told him Drake and I ran, but we later realized we had our own missions to finish. I had to come back and deliver the heart to Morda. And he had to go back, help Thomas, and win back his castle.

However, I also told him I became a slave, in some sense. I saw other slaves, how they were treated, how they lived, how they longed for a freedom they knew they would never have.

"The servants here are slaves," I said with a heavy heart. "I just had never realized it before."

He nodded. "It's not too bad … until the witches pick you for more than cleaning and hard labor."

My heart squeezed. I had barely made it a couple of weeks, and I had been treated well, thanks to Drake. I couldn't imagine living like this for a lifetime. "I'm sorry."

Shock shone in his dark eyes again. "You're really confusing, my lady."

I pointed my index finger at him. "Ah!"

"Sorry. Thea." One corner of his lips tugged up in a tiny smile.

"Why am I confusing?"

"Witches are cruel and evil and without remorse. You're a witch, and so far, you have been the kindest and honest person I have ever met. It's a contradiction."

His words weighed on me like heavy boulders. So this was how witches were viewed by others. All my life, I had thought witches were strong beings, women to be revered, adored, feared. Because we were so powerful, we knew what was best for everyone. We protected ours, even if that meant being violent toward others. It had always been like that.

It had never occurred to me that others might see us as cruel and evil. I had heard people say before we communed with the devil. I had thought it was ridiculous.

It made sense now. A curtain had been lifted from my eyes, from my mind and my soul. I could see it all now. We protected and fought for our family; we killed for those we loved, for what we loved. Witches loved power. Magic. Status.

Witches were evil and cruel.

Just like vampires were monsters.

Deja-vu.

Drake wasn't a monster, and I wasn't evil and cruel. If both of us weren't, there had to be others that weren't either. It wasn't all black and white anymore.

"I guess there are exceptions," I said, feeling confused too.

Keeran let out a long breath. "Thea, as much as I hate to suggest this, I guess you should consider taking me by force. Because if I don't sleep with you, Morda will kill me."

A lump rose to my throat. By all that was sacred ... "Don't worry, Keeran. She won't find out."

"How?"

It was now or never. "I haven't thought of all the details yet, but I plan to run away. You could come with me. You'll be free to do what you want, to live the way you desire."

His eyes widened and his face paled. "No, you can't. If you're caught ..."

"If I'm caught, I'll be punished. I know."

"No, no." He shook his head vehemently. "You don't understand. I guess you don't know because you weren't here."

"What don't I know?"

"While you were gone, Blackmarsh and Bluemoon attacked the Silverblood coven several times. Witches have gone missing, taken as slaves by the other covens, and there has been many deaths on both sides." He paused. "I heard rumors ..."

"Tell me."

"Lady Helen tried to escape. Princess Morda found her and punished her with the bloodbone ritual, to make an example out of her."

I gasped.

Helen had been another weak witch who volunteered for the suicide mission. She had been quiet like a little mouse, but I remembered seeing her in the halls and exchanging a few words with her during events. I would never guess she had the guts to leave.

And the bloodbone ritual ...

I closed my eyes as my stomach revolved thinking about it.

It didn't matter. Not really. I wouldn't let my fear of the ritual stop me from being with Drake.

"Don't worry," I said, more to myself than to him. "I will only leave when I'm certain I can do it." He was getting agitated with the subject, so I decided to change the topic. I stood. "It's getting late. Why don't you take my bed? You should rest so you can heal properly."

He stared at me with surprise written all over his features. "What about you?"

"I don't think I can sleep right now." I was tired to the bone, but my mind was worked up. Even if I lay down, I wouldn't be able to sleep. "Go." I beckoned toward my bed, then turned toward the door.

"Where are you going?" he asked.

I glanced over my shoulder. He was up and his body was coiled. He was wary again. "Don't worry. I'm going to find you some decent clothes and be right back. I promise." I shooed him away again. "Now go sleep."

I didn't wait for him to move before exiting the room. As I suspected, witchguards patrolled the hallways.

One of them stopped and faced me. I cleared my throat and put on a superior mask when I said, "Make sure my servant doesn't leave. I'm not finished with him yet."

The witchguard nodded.

Holding my head high, I strolled down the hallway. When I was out of sight, I let out a long breath.

I had to wear this mask for a few more hours. For a few more minutes. Because now, I was going to scout the mansion, to find out where Morda had posted witchguards and patrols, and prepare for my escape.

Tomorrow. Tomorrow, I would leave this place.

6

DRAKE

First, Alex had sent Luana to me, now he was ordering me to hunt a freaking werewolf. What was he trying to do? This wasn't about proving myself. There was much more going on. Alex was playing a game, and I had no option but to play along.

However, I didn't go alone. Alex sent Prince Phelps, Prince Gray, Eden, Ralf, and four other vampires with me.

"As witnesses," he said.

Which meant, if the werewolf were a strong one, stronger than me, and was about to kill me, the other vampires weren't supposed to intervene. They were there to watch, whatever the outcome.

I bet Alex was hoping it was a huge ass werewolf who could overpower me.

No matter. I would summon strength from hell if I needed it, but I wouldn't give him the satisfaction of seeing me gone. Not yet.

While I ran after the wolf into the woods, followed by the witnesses, Alex went to the balcony off Lord Reynard's office on the third floor—I guess it was Alex's office now. The thought disgusted me—to watch the hunt. Waiting for me screw up, I was sure.

The werewolf's scent was an odd one. It seemed masked, but I caught a faint trail and followed it, running as fast as I could. Werewolves were fast, but unless this one was the alpha, he couldn't outrun a five-hundred-year-old vampire.

The scent grew stronger. I was getting closer.

I ran into a valley and the scent died. I stopped in my tracks and turned, sniffing the air. The wolf was hiding. If I were human, I would have missed it in this darkness, but I focused on my enhanced sight and found it: a small opening in the side of the hill. It didn't look big enough for a cave, but it could be a burrow or a nest of some other animal.

The wolf was hiding inside.

I halted five feet from the entrance while the other vampires watched from a hill.

"Come out, little wolf, and I'll kill you quickly," I said in a normal voice, knowing he could hear me. I counted ten seconds before continuing. "Make me come after you and I'll drag your death out for days."

I gave him another ten seconds.

Damn it.

I took a step and—

The wolf lunged out of the burrow, right at me. Expecting such attack, I easily spun out of the way. The wolf landed where I had been just a moment before, and instantly, it turned to face me. He had an unusual color, light brown fur with some golden patches running down his paws and up his ears. His hazel eyes gleamed with vengeance.

I readied myself in a fighting stance—feet apart, weight on the back leg, hands up—and smiled at the creature. "I changed my mind. I'll take you alive so we can interrogate you. After all, I'd like to know why you were on DuMoir grounds."

The wolf snarled and charged at me again. I knelt and threw my arms out, connecting with his stomach. I pushed up hard, and the wolf let out a cry as he flipped over me and landed on his back behind me.

The wolf whimpered and rushed to his feet, but I was on him before he could recover. Fangs already out, I pushed him back down and bit him in the shoulder. I went for the joints, right where the ligaments connected with the muscles, but the wolf twisted and I ended up taking pure muscle. Regardless, I let out my poison. Even if this wolf got away, it would be dead in a couple of hours.

The wolf jerked and cried.

I pulled back enough to lean over him again and bite somewhere else, but the wolf thrashed under me. His paw connected with my shoulder, making me lose balance. And that was his opening.

The wolf thrashed some more until he was free of me.

The wolf's muscles trembled as he retreated. Where did he think he was going?

Irritated, I snarled at him. "I'm taking you down now." I went for him.

But he jumped out of the way. In an unexpected move, the wolf ran up the hill and lunged at Eden, who went down screaming.

Then, the wolf let him go and ran deeper into the woods.

I stared at Eden's body on the ground, not knowing what to do. Phelps and Gray knelt beside Eden, who was not dead, just down for the count.

Ralf glared at me. "What do you think you're doing? Go after the damn wolf!"

Hell.

I took off while the others stayed behind to help Eden.

This time, it was easier to follow the wolf since his scent was stronger with the open wound and blood, and because it was injured, it was slower.

Not even two minutes later, I spotted the wolf turning in the woods and going for the hills that marked the end of the DuMoir estate. Even if I didn't catch him before he reached the top of the hill, there were only fields and hills and valleys beyond our borders. He would be easy to spot.

The wolf reached the base of the hill and I sprinted, wanting to end this. By my estimate, the wolf would be crossing down the other side of the hill when I caught with him.

The wolf was on top of the hill when the clouds moved and covered the moon.

And the wolf turned into a woman.

I faltered in my step then shook my head, getting rid of the shock. I advanced toward the woman without rush—in this form, she was almost as slow as a human.

As I got closer, her odd scent became clearer.

She stumbled on her feet and fell on the ground.

Holding my breath, I moved toward her.

Luana.

She curled into herself, hiding her body from view, but I wasn't paying attention to that. I was speechless, because I hadn't even considered the werewolf could be a woman and that woman would be my new blood slave. More importantly, now that she wasn't covered in fur, I could see her injury. I had torn part of her muscle and blood flowed freely down her naked body.

"Just kill me," she whispered, closing her eyes.

I knelt beside her, took off my shirt, and covered her body with it. "How were you ...?"

"It's a long story."

"We have time." I had no idea if the other vampires were on our trail, or if they would come at all, but I hoped they took their sweet time if they did. She pushed up, but her arms gave out. I reached for her and she cried out in pain as I helped her sit up. Shit. I ripped a piece of the shirt sleeves and tied it around her arm. It wouldn't fix her arm or stop the bleeding, but it would slow it down. "Now, explain yourself before I finish what I started."

"Don't look," she muttered, and I turned my face as she slipped my shirt on. "You can look now." She was closing up the buttons of the once white shirt. It was now mostly bright red with her blood.

"And you can talk now."

She took in a wavering breath. "I don't know where to start."

"How about how and why you were at DuMoir Castle?"

"I was captured by Prince Alex and his men a couple of weeks ago while I was scoping out the castle," she said, her eyes filling with tears.

"Scoping the castle? Why? Do the werewolves plan on attacking?"

She shrugged her good shoulder. "If there was an opportunity, I believe so. My pack leader sends a wolf out every once in a while to check how things are going."

"But you didn't report back because you were caught."

"Right. I changed into my human form before Alex and

his men caught me, and they assumed I was a lost human. How they didn't smell the wolf in me, I don't know." Even though I had found her scent odd, I also hadn't noticed she was a werewolf. "I was immediately brought to the slave quarters and locked in there." She wiped her eyes with her good arm. "I wanted to escape, but I wasn't even allowed outside. So, I came up with another plan. I had heard rumors that you were good to your blood slaves. You were more lenient and didn't abuse them. I thought ... I thought that if I became your blood slave, it would be easier for me to escape." Stupid girl. "So I started working on Prince Patrick, the one who called on me the most, about becoming your blood slave. But then Thea appeared and you ran away with her, so I to change my plan."

"But now I'm back."

"Yes. I heard you were back and I heard Prince—*Lord*—Alex talking to a few princes about taunting you with a new blood slave. He said it would drive you crazy to have one delivered to you right after losing Thea and Thomas."

My stomach tightened. He was damn right. Shit. "And?"

"I volunteered. Of course Lord Alex asked me to report your activities to him. In return, he would provide me with treasure."

I scoffed. "You believed him?"

"Of course not. But it was my opportunity to be your blood slave."

My jaw ticked. "When I told you to leave me alone a couple of hours ago, you left not only my bedroom, but my chambers."

"You're the only prince without several slaves in every corner of their chambers, working like crazy. It was easy sneaking out through the door connecting the kitchens."

"You were going back to your pack."

"If I make it there." Luana glanced down to her ripped arm. The bleeding slowed, but if we didn't stop it soon, she would bleed out. Not to mention the poison.

"Do you have healers who can pull out a vampire's poison?"

"I think so." Her eyes widened. "You're letting me go?"

"I might. But first we need to talk."

She groaned. "Do it fast before I die here."

I wasn't sure if she was attempting to joke around her dreadful situation or if she was serious.

"I want to overthrow Alex and take DuMoir Castle."

"What? How? Why?"

I chuckled. "I'll start with why. Because Alex is a bastard and he'll destroy our world. He'll destroy all humans, to start, then he'll come after the other supernaturals."

"And how would it be different if you were in charge?"

"For one, I don't want to be in charge, but someone has to be, and so far, I haven't found many people who share my beliefs."

"What beliefs?"

"That all races can coexist without declaring war every five minutes."

She stared at me for a long time. "I like that."

"As for the how, that's where you come in."

I explained to her that I was sure I could find a dozen allies inside the castle, but that wasn't enough against the other hundreds. I needed allies, and if her pack was willing, I would ask for their help in bringing Alex down. In exchange, we would draw up a nice peace treaty. No more hunting of both races.

"I like this, but I don't have authority to answer for my

alpha," she said. "As it is, he probably thinks I'm dead right now."

"Then go to your pack. Get healed, talk to your alpha, and then come back with a message."

She stared at me. "Just like that."

"Just like that."

"How are you gonna come back now empty-handed?"

"I'll go deeper into the woods, kill a random wolf, and tell him it's a werewolf."

"Alex might not buy it."

"I'm hoping he will."

"There's too much leaning on hope here."

I nodded. "Unfortunately, that's all we have."

Luana and I agreed she would sneak back into the castle after she talked to her pack and the full moon was gone—apparently, she wasn't mated yet. Unmated female wolves were weaker and couldn't control the change under the full moon.

I re-tied the piece of cloth around her arm, making it tighter so she wouldn't bleed out before reaching her destination, and watched as she stumbled downhill, toward her pack.

I stayed there under the cloudy skies, thinking of Thea and Luana and the plan that was forming. Hell, I hoped it worked.

Letting out a long breath, I turned around and ran into the woods. I had a wolf to kill.

7

THEA

A KNOCK WOKE ME UP. STARTLED, I ROLLED AND ALMOST FELL to the ground.

Where was I? What was happening?

In a flash, my mind caught up and I remembered every-thing. I was back in the Silverblood coven, in my bedroom, with a servant in my bed, and I probably only slept a couple of hours since I was now required to go to back to normal daylight hours.

The knock came again, and Keeran showed up in front of me, still wearing the loincloth-skirt-thing. "I'll get it," he said.

I started protesting, and then remembered he was supposed to be my servant.

I had time to run around the love seat to the bed before Keeran opened the door, revealing a witchguard on the other side.

Keeran stepped to the side.

"What is it?" I asked.

"Princess Morda requests your presence for breakfast in

thirty minutes," the witchguard said. Without ceremony, she marched away and Keeran closed the door.

I sat at the edge of the bed. "Breakfast," I mused, surprised.

Breakfast with Morda and her inner circle was an honor only a few witches experienced. Of course, I wasn't one. Until now. I wondered why she had invited me. It was probably because I had succeeded and brought back the coven's heart. Now, she wanted to show the other witches how benevolent and fair she was by being kind to me and inviting me to events, like breakfast with her.

I felt sick at the thought that I was one more pawn in Morda's game, and I confess I considered not going. But I couldn't refuse her. Not yet.

Feeling like I was going on another mission, I turned to Keeran and said, "Let's get ready."

He raised an eyebrow. "Let's ...?"

"Witches take their servants to breakfast. You're my servant now, so I have to show you off." I gestured to the small bag on the side of the bed. "I got you some clothes. Nothing much but better than ..." I pointed a finger at him. "That."

I took a shower first and got dressed. Knowing Morda liked her witches to be well dressed, I choose a long but casual black dress. While I applied some makeup and brushed my long hair, Keeran took his turn in the bathroom. When he emerged, his short hair was brushed back and clean, and he wore the gray pants and white shirt I had gotten him. My mouth fell open. He was miles away from the man who had been in a loincloth last night. That man had been broken, cowering, hurt. His shoulders had sagged, and he couldn't lift his chin to look at me. I was sure he still felt all that inside, but the man standing before me now? He looked handsome, imposing, and strong.

I smiled. "You clean up well."

His golden cheeks gained a faint red tint. "Are you sure you want me to go?"

"It's more like I need you to go," I said, beckoning him to come to me. Once he halted in front of me, I hooked my arm on his. "Are you ready?"

"Can I answer that honestly?"

Right. He hated witches. He feared them. Of course, he wasn't ready. To be honest, I wasn't feeling ready either. But if we waited any longer, we would be late, and Morda would show off her short temper. Living in the Silverblood mansion was an endless game. And right now, I was a big player.

Only until tonight, though, because tonight I was leaving.

"Let's go," I said in a low voice.

Breakfast with Morda and her inner circle was held in a private dining room inside Morda's quarters. An elegant room with off-white stone flooring, light gray walls, and a long glass table housing twenty chairs.

When we arrived, most of the witches were standing around the table, and their servants stood by the walls, all waiting for Morda, who, it was said, only came in once everyone had arrived.

I immediately saw Soraya, Liliana, Adya, Polina, and Vera. They all wrinkled their noses at me.

Two witchguards burst into the room through an archway and positioned themselves by the wall, their enchanted escrima sticks in hand. Not five seconds later, Princess Morda walked in, looking powerful in her long, fluffy, dark gray gown.

"Please, sit down," she said in her firm tone.

Only after Morda took the chair at the head of the table did the other witches sit . Soraya sat to her right; Adya sat to her left. The rest spread out on the long table. I ended up in the middle, squeezed between Liliana and Polina.

Male servants, dressed in gray pants and sporting naked chests, brought out the food and set it around the table. There was everything to choose from—sour bread, sweet bread, cakes, pancakes, waffles, eggs of all kinds, bacon, ham, salami, smoked salmon, croissants and other pastries, fruits, porridge, and more. As for drink, there were at least eight kinds of juice, coffee, tea, sparkling water, and even wine and champagne. It was a feast.

Imitating the other handful of servants in the room, Keeran came forward and served me: a piece of cake, a slice of bread with blueberry jelly, some smoked salmon, an apple, and grape juice.

Everything looked delicious, and I was ready to dig in.

"I've heard so much about you," Vera said from across the table.

"Oh, me too," Polina said, turning to me. "What a feat! You went to the most powerful vampire coven around and succeeded."

"Tell us about it," Adya asked.

And just like that, I lost my appetite. I glanced at Morda, and sure enough, she was watching me. "I don't think our host would appreciate hearing the gory details over such a nice breakfast."

Morda tsked. "Oh, go ahead. Give them all the juicy details."

I hadn't even told her the juicy details. In fact, I couldn't tell them all of the details. They couldn't know how Drake had claimed me, how we got close, how I ended up falling in love with him, how I was willing to sacrifice everything for him.

Staring at me, Soraya leaned on her elbows and steepled her fingers. "So?"

I took in a sharp breath. "There's nothing much to tell. I was accepted for the tour and was prepared when the vampires attacked in the ballroom. However, Lord Reynard was killed."

"That's quite intriguing," Morda muttered. She nodded at me. "Go on."

"It all became a little chaotic because the vampires weren't expecting it." So far no lies. But they all started now. "I was taken with the other blood slaves saved for later, but soon realized I wouldn't be able to look for the coven's heart if I was locked away. So, when one of the princes wanted a new blood slave, I did my best to be chosen."

"So you were bitten by a vampire?" Liliana asked.

"How was it?" Adya asked.

"Did it hurt?" Vera asked.

"No, no," I added quickly. Also a lie, but I had only been bitten by Drake because I had allowed him to. "To my surprise, the prince only wanted company." For some reason, I didn't want them to assume I had been bitten or raped by the vampires. However, Morda's frown told me she wasn't happy about that. Whatever. "I had some freedom with him, which was perfect. The princes had instilled a ten-day mourning period following Lord Reynard's death, so the castle was quiet. It was easier to roam around. I sneaked into Lord Reynard's office and found out where he was keeping the coven's heart." The rest was mostly the truth. I told them about finding Lord Reynard's treasure room, about being attacked by Sarki, about killing her, and the fighting. "With the heart's power, I was able to fight my way out of the castle. The vampires pursued me, but I escaped." I stared at Morda. "A few hours later, you found me."

"Wow, that is quite the tale," Liliana said.

"I can't believe you did all that," Adya said.

"Quite the hero," Polina said.

Wait … did they? … No. They didn't. They couldn't. What, now I was some kind of legend for having survived DuMoir Castle and bringing back the heart? That was crazy.

"Thea," Morda started. "We should meet later and discuss some things about the vampires."

My stomach clenched. What did she want to know? Did she doubt me? Did she see through my facade? "Of course," I forced out, feeling incredible vulnerable.

She glanced to the wall behind me, and I was sure she was looking at Keeran. Then, she returned her cool gaze to me and asked, "Was the servant I sent you enough to satisfy you? Or should I send another man? Or perhaps *men*?"

"No, no," I sputtered. "No need. I'm quite well with Keeran. In fact …" I cleared my throat and forced my fake bravado out, the same one I had used so many times on Drake. "I was wondering if I could keep him to myself. You know, at least for a while."

I did not intend to touch him, but if he stayed by my side, he would be safe. At least until I left tonight—if I didn't convince him to run away with me.

A wicked smile stretched over Morda's lips. "Because you brought the heart back, I'll grant you one reward. Do you want Keeran as your reward?"

"Yes," I said, no hesitation.

She stood from her chair and took two steps back. "Come

here." Dread filled me. Slowly, I rose from my chair and went to her. She looked at Keeran. "You too."

Keeran's face paled, but he held his head high as he approached us. "Yes, your highness?" he asked, bowing to her.

Morda grasped my wrist and Keeran's and joined our hands. His eyes locked on mine, and I was sure mine reflected the apprehension stamped on his. Morda placed both her hands over ours. A bright light shone from her palms, warming my skin and sending a jolt over my arm, to my chest.

I gasped and Keeran coughed.

Morda dropped her hands. "Done."

"Your highness?" I asked, confused.

"I've bonded you two," she said, as if it were the most normal thing in the world. "Now, you two can't be apart for more than a short time, otherwise the servant will hurt, and no other witch may touch your servant without being burned." I gaped at her. By all that was sacred, what had she done? "You're welcome," she said with a smile.

"T-thank you, your highness," I said, my voice barely above a whisper.

Ignoring Keeran and me, Morda faced the other witches at the table. "We'll soon have a meeting where I'll inspect each of you." She stared at the witches, me included. "I'll use my magic for a pregnancy test. If you're not all pregnant by then, you'll be punished. No, actually, I might execute you."

A chill ran down my spine.

After dropping a bomb like that, Morda picked up the hem of her gown, spun around, and sauntered out of the dining room.

Whispers rose from the table along with the witches.

Some of them gathered, all talking about the upcoming pregnancy check.

Meanwhile, my heart thundered in my chest. Pregnancy check? By all that was sacred, how would I get pregnant? If I had to, there was only one man I would sleep with, and right now, he was too far away.

Keeran stepped closer me. "Thea, about this bonding spell ..."

"Not here," I whispered. We couldn't risk anyone hearing us. "Let's go back to my bedroom."

We left Morda's chambers and walked by one of the groups in the hallway. At first, I didn't pay any attention to them—they were probably worried about getting pregnant and letting out their frustrations—but then I noticed Ebby, a weak witch I hadn't seen in a while, was right in the middle and her eyes were full of tears.

My step faltered.

"What are you doing here?" one witch asked her, her voice dripping with disdain.

"I-I was just walking by," Ebby said in a trembling tone. I hadn't been close to her, but I remembered she being even weaker than I was before I left for my mission. She had always been teased and bullied by the other witches. It seemed nothing had changed.

"Why?" another witch asked. "There's only Princess Morda's chambers on this side of the mansion."

"She must have tried to sneak in."

"Maybe she tried using a spell to sneak in."

"Maybe she was trying to cast a spell to have Princess Morda like her."

"Morda is too strong to be affected by a spell like that. It must be something else."

One of the witches poked her in the shoulder. "What did you do? Which spell did you use?" She pushed Ebby back again, causing her to trip on her feet.

I clenched my fists and stepped into the group. "Excuse me," I said, my voice loud and clear. The witches stared at me with confusion and reservation across their features. They practically idolized me. I had to use that to my advantage. I flipped my hair and lifted my chin high. "Would you mind if I have a word with Ebby? I need to discuss an important matter with her." The witches exchanged nervous stares. "I hope that is okay," I insisted, putting a hard edge to my voice.

"S-sure," one of the witches said. Together, the witches scurried away.

I hooked my arm on Ebby's and pulled her farther down the hallway, away from everyone else.

"Are you okay?" I asked her in a whisper.

She stared at me with her big green eyes. "Why do you care?"

I flinched, not expecting that reaction from her. "I was trying to help."

She wiped at her eyes. "I don't need your help." She humphed before scurrying away.

I stared after her. Poor girl. She was probably so used to everyone picking on her, that she didn't know what to do when someone was kind to her.

Shaking my head, I resumed my walk with Keeran close on my heels.

Once we were safe inside my bedroom, Keeran took a vase-like position along the wall, and I sank on the love seat, trying to process all that had happened in such a short time.

What now?

Now that Morda had bonded me to Keeran, I couldn't run

away without him. And if I didn't run away, Morda would perform the pregnancy test on me and I would fail it. She would kill me.

I wasn't ready to die.

I looked at Keeran. But I also wasn't ready to sleep with another man. I guess I would never be. My heart, body, and soul belonged to Drake.

Unless ...

"Thank you," Keeran said. He was still against the wall, but his eyes were full of emotion. "I know you told Morda you wanted me to stay with you to protect me from the other witches." He pressed his lips together. "I'm sorry it backfired. I'm sorry you're bonded to me now."

"It's not your fault," I said. "But I need a favor from you."

He took two steps closer. "Anything."

My mind set, I rose, grabbed a notebook and pen from the drawer in one of my nightstands, sat on the edge of my bed, and wrote a quick note.

I folded the note and handed it to Keeran. "Here."

Brows curled down, he took the note. "Who is it for?"

It wouldn't be easy, but it was the only choice I could think of.

Finally, I said, "Drake."

8

———

DRAKE

I GOT BACK TO THE CASTLE A LITTLE BEFORE MIDNIGHT.

"There you are," Luana said once I entered my chambers.

I was surprised to see her. I thought she wouldn't be back for a couple of days. "When did you get back?"

"About three hours ago," she said, looking a little mad at me. "It was a little tricky to get back into the castle, but here I am. Though, when I got here and didn't find you, I thought ..."

"What?"

"That Alex had found out about your lie and killed you."

"If they had examined the wolf, they would have caught me, but they didn't even care."

When delivering the fake werewolf, I had been on edge, but Alex and the princes bought it. Alex was still looking for a way to get to me, though. I glanced at her arm. It looked perfect fine.

"I see your arm is healed and you're well. I'm glad."

"Thankfully, the healer in my pack is experienced." She

looked at me, at my clothes, probably finding my sweatpants and a Henley as weird as I felt wearing them. "Where have you been?"

"I was running an errand," I said. She didn't need to know where I had gone. No one did. "So, did you talk to your alpha?"

"Yes." She lifted her chin high, reminded me of Thea. A pang cut through my chest. "His name is Ulric, and he wants to meet you in two nights."

"He'll help me?"

"Right now, he'll meet you so you can plead your case."

"Fair enough." I sighed. Then, I finally took in her attire. A long, black dress. "Where are you going?"

"You mean, where are *we* going?" she said. "A little while ago, you received an invitation from Lord Alex for a formal banquet in the ballroom. It starts in fifteen minutes."

I ran a hand through my hair. "Hell ..." After running for hours, my muscles groaned and I could use a bottle of blood. All I wanted was nourishment and rest. I didn't feel like going anywhere. But once more, I had no choice here.

"I'll get ready." I started toward my bedroom, but stopped and looked at Luana. "If you're going with me as my blood slave, then find another dress. Something more revealing. Something red and provocative."

A knot appeared between her brows. "Why?"

"So Alex and the princes buy that I'm into you and have forgotten all about Thea."

I couldn't read the emotion that flashed in her eyes before she showed me indifference again. Shrugging her shoulders, she marched to her bedroom. And I went to mine to get ready.

I could have used a long bath, but settled for a quick shower. After putting on my formal clothes—black tuxedo, dark red shirt, and black tie—I went back to the living room.

"Is this better?" Standing in front of the sofa, Luana spun around. A dark red dress with a low neckline, tight torso, lace around her midriff, and a long slit up the side of her legs.

"Much better," I said, realizing she was prettier than I first realized.

"I was hoping you would say no." Groaning, she hugged herself, hiding her waist. "I really don't like this dress."

"You'll be fine. All you have to do is put on a show."

She groaned again. "Another thing I don't want to do."

I scoffed. "We all do things we don't want to. For example, I'm here, aren't I? Though I wish I weren't." I offered my arm to her. "Let's go."

Rolling her eyes, Luana rested her hand on the inside of my elbow, and together, we walked down to the ballroom.

While approaching the entrance, a thought occurred to me. Alex hadn't stripped me of my title, but he had taken everything that came with it. Did that mean I was supposed to use the entrance on the main level, or could I still use the royalty entrance atop the balcony?

To irk him, I chose to go through the same place I always had. With Luana by my side.

When we entered the ballroom, Alex and all the princes were already on the landing, looking down at the guests.

Wait, guests?

The air rushed out of me once I realized the place was filled with humans.

I halted beside the other princes, but before I could ask what was going on, Alex opened his arms high and shouted, "Let's feast."

The vampires positioned along the walls lunged at the human guests, who as usual were too dazed, too drugged to react. No one screamed, no one cried, while the vampires bit their necks and drank their blood.

Behind me, Luana's heart sped up and her hands closed tight around my arm.

Alex, who stood at the edge of the stairs, glanced over his shoulder at us. "Go on, princes. Feast."

Without hesitation, the princes—Dorian, Aston, Nolan, Patrick, Cain, Gray, and Phelps—jumped off the landing and grabbed a human or two for themselves.

My stomach turned.

A satisfied grin took over Alex's features. "Aren't you going to feast, Prince Drake?" He looked at Luana. "Or is your new pet keeping your satisfied?"

"What are you doing, Alex?"

"Lord Alex," he rasped, clearly irritated. "I'm doing what we should have been doing for centuries now. Bringing humans to the castle once a month instead of twice a year. Why almost starve ourselves when we are stronger, faster, better?"

I clenched my teeth. "Did you talk to the princes about this?"

"Are you jealous you aren't included in such decisions anymore?"

I didn't dignify him with an answer, but my silence was enough.

To be honest, I wasn't jealous. I was disappointed. Maybe if I had been there, if I could have uttered my vote, the ruling would have leaned the other way. Maybe we wouldn't be massacring humans for Alex's pleasure.

"The princes barely had any say in this," he continued.

"Now that I'm Lord of the castle, I do what I want."

That was so goddamn wrong …

"That isn't how things are done here," I said. When Lord Reynard ruled, he always listened to his princes, and before important decisions, he always held a vote to make sure it was fair.

"It is now," he snarled. "Don't you forget, Prince Drake. You are here, alive and kicking, because I'm allowing you to be. I can end you—" He snapped his fingers. "—just like that."

I didn't dare tell him he was dreaming. I was older than he was, only by a couple of decades, but that meant I was stronger. If we ever dueled, I would kick his sorry ass from here to the moon and back.

Instead, I gritted my teeth, clenched my hands, and held his defiant stare.

He let out a laugh. "I see you continue to be no fun." He patted my shoulder, but I jerked away. "Go feast, prince, before I change my mind and take even that privilege from you."

With that, he spun around and jumped, floating to the floor below where the humans awaited their end.

I stared, disgusted by such a sight. What had Alex done? The potion in the humans' drinks had to be stronger this time for them to act like that—swaying as if they were dancing, chatting, and laughing as if they were at a real party. And not one bit aware of the massacre surrounding them.

There had to be at least fifty humans here, and half had already become corpses littering the floor. It was then I realized Alex didn't intend to leave any humans alive for later. The vampires would kill them all.

I reached behind me and grabbed Luana's hand. "Let's get out of here," I whispered.

She didn't object as I pulled her out of the ballroom.

The hallways were practically empty, but I could hear Luana's heart hammering as if it were a church bell echoing off the walls.

Once we were inside my chambers, I pushed her down on the couch and knelt beside her. "Are you okay?"

Wide and filled with tears, she turned her eyes to me. "W-was that the legendary bi-annual feast?"

I sighed. "Yes, but apparently, Alex now wants to make it a monthly occurrence."

"That was horrible," she whispered. "Since I had been found outside the castle, I was put down in the blood slaves' quarters. I had heard about the feast, of course, but had never seen it." She pressed a hand against her chest. "I can't … Those people … Oh, my heart."

"I know, I know." I rose and paced around the living room, too agitated, too angry to settle. "I never liked them. In fact, I hated them." I had always suggested we do something else for blood. Like the damn hospital bags we bought to fill our bottles. We could live off that, for sure. But no one ever wanted that. They enjoyed the warm blood from humans, even if it was only once every so often. They also enjoyed the thrill, the game, the hunt. But now … now Alex had gone overboard. Once a month? That was too much.

Luana clenched her fists. She lifted her head, blinking her eyes fast as if fighting tears—and exposing her long neck. Her heart still beat too fast and I could see, and hear, the vein in her beck thrumming.

Even though I didn't want to, I couldn't deny having her in here was too much right now.

Hell, I needed to get out of here.

Trying to ignore her odd scent and the sound of her blood rushing through her veins, I turned to the door.

"Where are you going?" Luana asked, her voice breaking.

"I ... I'll be back later." I paused at the door, but didn't look at her as I said, "Don't leave. It's not safe right now."

I rushed down to the back garden, and inhaled a lungful of fresh air as I walked away from the castle.

Shit.

What the hell had come over me?

Well, it wasn't the first time I had been tempted into drinking from a human during a feast—or after in this case. And I hated to admit it, but it happened more often than I was comfortable with.

I blamed the fact that I had been a pile of anger after talking to Alex during the feast. That and missing Thea. Those two facts put me over the edge, and I was suddenly ready to drink from a werewolf.

I was glad to see I could control myself and get away from her before I did anything.

I halted in front of the bench where I had first kissed Thea. I hadn't even realized I was coming this way, but now that I was here, I could understand why. I missed her. Plain and simple. It had been only a couple of days since we separated, and yet I missed her so much, it hurt.

I sat on the bench and closed my eyes. Images of Thea and our time together flashed through my mind. I held on to them, willing them to give me strength so I could endure this forsaken mission.

Why the hell did I feel this immense, painful necessity to make everything right? To bring justice to this place, and save this castle? Why the hell did I care so much?

The fall of a soft footstep reached my ears, and a few seconds later, I caught a new scent in the air.

My eyes snapped open, and I went on full alert.

Who was spying on me now?

Slowly, I rose and followed the faint scent trail, careful so I would keep hidden and find the vampire before he found me. The scent got stronger the closer I got, and I soon realized whoever was coming wasn't a vampire.

It was a human.

I found the human, a man in his early twenties, keeping to the shadows in the garden and creeping closer to the mansion.

I came up right behind him. "What are you doing here?"

Startled, the man turned to me, a knife in his hand. "Don't come any closer."

Could he be a human who escaped the feast? And why was he going toward the castle and not away from it? "What are you doing here?"

The man's eyes widened. "I-I'm looking for someone. A vampire. I was told he likes to roam the gardens alone. Drake is his name."

What ...? How ...? My hunger had subsided, but I elongated my fangs for show. "Who are you, and what do you want with Drake?"

The man's arm trembled, but he kept that blade poised at my chest. As if that could stop me from breaking his neck. "I have something to tell him."

"Who are you?" I snarled, showing off my fangs.

The man took a step back. "You're him, right? You're Drake. I know because Thea told me about you."

My fangs retreated and my shoulders sagged. "Thea? What about Thea? Is she okay? Where is she?"

The man didn't lower the dagger as he said, "I'm Keeran, Thea's servant."

Thea had a servant? Despite myself, I looked at him with different eyes. The man was good-looking for a human and was wearing nice clothes for a servant. I didn't like it. "Why are you here?"

"She asked me to hand you this." With his free hand, Keeran fished a folded paper from his pocket. I took the paper from him and cradled it in my mind as if it were worth my weight in gold. Groaning, Keeran slapped a hand over his chest. "I need to go now," he muttered. "I can't stay away for long or the spell might kill me."

What did that mean? But before I could ask, the man walked away.

"Thank you," I said, loud enough so he could hear.

Keeran tipped his head once, and then took off.

I stared at the spot he had been with my senses focused on our surroundings to make sure no one else, vampire or human, was around. When he was out of range, I glanced at the note.

Thea had risked the life of her servant to send me this note. It was probably important. And yet, I was finding it hard to open it.

Instead, jealousy festered in my chest. Why hadn't Thea told me she had a servant? A male one? A good-looking male servant? Had she been afraid I would be jealous? Be jealous and angry?

I sighed. Who was I to talk? I now had a new blood slave I hadn't asked for, and she was pretty for a werewolf.

This was stupid. I loved Thea and I hoped she knew that. I wanted her to trust me, to trust my feelings for her, so I had to do the same.

I trusted her.

With that in mind, I unfolded the note.

Meet me at the place we parted at midnight tomorrow.

9

THEA

"Are you sure about this?" Keeran asked for the hundredth time.

"I have to go," I said as I folded my black cloak over my arm. "I told him I would be there, so I better be there."

"What if he doesn't go? What if he can't go?"

"It's a risk I have to take." I placed my hand on his arm. "Relax, Keeran. It'll be alright."

"I don't like this," he said. Another sentence he had repeated often this evening.

We had talked about the details earlier, and he seemed okay with it, but now he was nervous. I was too—my stomach was tied in knots—but I wouldn't let that stop me from meeting Drake.

As agreed, Keeran would stay in my bedroom. If someone came to see me, he would tell them I was in the bathroom, soaking in a bath and didn't want to be disrupted. If it was urgent or an order from Morda, I would deal with the consequences later. However, I was going out at midnight. The castle would be quieter. Nobody would come to see me until at least tomorrow morning.

I also promised Keeran I wouldn't stay away long, so the bond wouldn't hurt him.

I turned to the door. "See you later."

"Please, be careful," Keeran said.

I smiled at him over my shoulder. "Don't worry."

I slipped out of my bedroom.

As expected, there were a couple of witchguards patrolling, but I was able to dodge them —using magic, of course.

I was ten feet from one of the mansion's side entrances when I heard sniffles. I frowned, berating myself for caring, but unable to stop as I stepped closer to the sound.

Ebby sat in the shadows of one of the narrow staircases used by servants, crying her eyes out.

When she saw me, she brought her arm up and turned her face so I couldn't see her.

The thought of leaving her crossed my mind; she had refused my help before. I also didn't want to be late to meet Drake, but guilt snaked around my heart and I couldn't. I could spare her a few minutes.

I squeezed in beside her. "What happened?" She wiped her face, but didn't answer me. "I can see there's something wrong, and apparently, you can't solve your problem alone. I can only help if you talk to me."

She looked at me from the corner of her eyes. "Why do you want to help?"

I snorted. Good question. "Because I was in your shoes not too long ago." In truth, I didn't remember cowering in the corners and crying that much, but I had been teased by the other witches and that had hurt me.

"You're popular now," she said, her voice low. "You're one of Princess Morda's favorites."

"Can I tell you a secret?" Her eyes widened and she nodded. "My suicide mission? I only got away because I was lucky. It wasn't skill; it wasn't because I'm special or powerful, or whatever. It was pure luck."

"Then I guess I need a suicide mission and a good amount of luck on my side." Her tone was lighter, as if she were trying to joke.

"Please, don't. Luck is hard to come by. However, we can bring luck to your side."

"How?"

"By making you a better witch." I smiled at her, hoping it was warm and caring enough. "If you want, I can practice some spells with you. We can start with some basic ones and build up from there. I bet that with the proper practice and a caring instructor, you'll be a stronger witch in no time." I didn't remind her of the fact that the heart was now back, and it would make all of us stronger. She didn't need to know that. It was better if she believed she was stronger by her own doing. "What do you think?"

She immediately perked up. "Can we start now? Right now?"

My smile fell. "Now? I'm sorry, but I can't. I have ... a quick errand to run and I'm dead tired." I could see her entire body tensing. "But we can do it tomorrow. I promise."

"I knew it," she yelled, standing up. "You're teasing me like the others. First you reach out to me, get my hopes up, and then shut me down to laugh in my face."

"Ebby, no, tha—"

"Shut up!" She clenched her fists. "And to think I almost fell for it."

Ebby stormed off before I could assure her I wasn't joking. I wanted to help her, but right now? Right now, I couldn't. I couldn't even go after her to tell her that I was serious, or I would be late.

My heart yanked at the prospect of leaving Ebby in that state, but it also yearned for what was waiting for me.

Letting out a long sigh, I put on my cloak, pulled the hood up, and ran out of the mansion.

Even though I used magic to make me faster, it took me almost an hour to get to the cottage where I had last seen Drake, but I made it with a minute to spare.

My hands trembled as I pushed through the front door and entered the place. "Drake?" I called out. The place was dark, but that was to be expected. I doubted Drake would turn on all the lights while waiting for me. But as I roamed the place, I realized he wasn't here.

I didn't let myself consider the fact that he might not come. Instead, I sat down on the couch close to the window, where I had a good view from the front porch and waited, sure he was late because he had a hard time getting away from the castle.

But as the minutes passed, my heart wilted.

An hour later, I was fighting back tears. What should I do? Should I wait? Should I go back to my coven before sunrise? Why wasn't he here yet? Did he have a hard time getting away, or was he not coming at all? If he wasn't coming, was it because Alex and the others were keeping him busy, or was it because he didn't love me anymore?

I shook my head, pushing away those thoughts.

Drake still loved me. It had been only a handful of days since we last saw each other. His heart couldn't have changed so fast.

Still, as I rose and picked up my cloak, I felt my heart breaking. I was so sure I was going to see him, to talk to him, to touch him that the idea of leaving without hearing from him made me sick. But I couldn't stay forever.

With my heart in pieces, I wrapped the cloak around my shoulders and stepped out of the cottage.

And right into Drake's arms.

"Where do you think you're going?" he asked, his eyes boring holes into mine.

I froze, not believing he was here. I grabbed his shoulders, testing it out. By all that was sacred, he was here. "You came," I whispered.

His arms tightened around my waist, gluing my body to his. "Sorry I'm late."

Drake's mouth fell over mine, and while holding me and kissing me, he walked into the cottage and closed the door behind us. He whirled us around and pushed me against the wall.

One of his hands flew to my neck, the other cupped my butt. His soft lips moved in rhythm with mine, wanting more, asking for every ounce of life and energy. His tongue invaded my mouth and entangled with mine.

Drake pulled my hair, making me tilt my head back as he traced my neck with his tongue, sending searing twinges through my skin. The heat spread through my body and lodged between my legs. I needed him. I wanted him.

I brushed my hips against his; I broke the kiss and whispered in his ear, "Take me."

Desire flashed in his eyes before his mouth claimed mine again, and I melted into it, intoxicated by his scent, by his touch, by his kiss. In seconds, Drake got rid of our clothes, and with his hands on my hips and his eyes locked on mine, he entered me. I moaned, a merry jolt traveling up my spine, as he filled me and thrust his hips against mine, coming fast and deep and making me dizzy in a sea of pure pleasure.

"Hell," he whispered before kissing me again. I sank my nails in his back, pulling him to me, making sure he would never leave. One of his hands slid up my stomach and cupped my breast. With his thumb, he grazed my nipple, stimulating it, making it hard and sending more jolts of pleasure through my body.

"Yes," I whispered as he plunged harder, touching me in ways and places I had never been touched before. Could this be possible? Yet, I wanted more of him. I wanted all of him. I raised my legs, twined them around his waist, and arched my back, helping him go even deeper. "Yes," I cried as shivers ran down my body, making my limbs tingle. "That's it."

Drake's fingers pinched my nipple, his other hand clasped my butt, making sure I was close, and he bit my lips. "Like that?" he whispered, thrusting more rapidly. And that was all it took. I peaked and trembled in his arms. His thrusts never easing off. I leaned into him, savoring each second of my blissful trance. His grip on me tightened, and after a final stout stroke, Drake exploded. He pressed me firmer against the wall as the ecstasy spams ran through his body.

With a satisfied smile, I slid my arms around his neck and kissed him. His lips moved with mine, pressing me as if we could melt into each other, until his spams lessened and died out.

Gently, Drake carried me to the bed, where he laid me down, before lying beside me.

"That wasn't exactly what I had in mind," he said, eyeing the ceiling.

I rolled halfway over him. "And what did you have in mind?"

He chuckled. "I mean, of course, I wanted to make love to you again, but I thought we would take it slow …"

I smiled. "Maybe we were frantic because it was the first time we had seen each other since we were separated."

"I think you're right."

My smile faded. "Aren't you wondering why I called you here?"

He raised an eyebrow. "I thought the reason was pretty clear."

I slapped his shoulder and he chuckled. "Well, there's more. It's related to that, but there's more."

He smoothed his hand down my back, and I had to push down the feelings his touch awoke inside me. "Then what is it?"

I sat up, unsure how he would receive this news. "Morda ordered all our witches to get pregnant." I paused, hoping it sank in. He stared at me, clearly confused. "Including me. I'm supposed to get pregnant."

10

DRAKE

I stared at Thea.

"Did you hear me?" she asked.

"Yes," I said.

"Do you know what that means?"

I nodded. "Yes."

"Say something else," she said, her voice gaining a worried tone. "Say more than yes."

"You said you have to get pregnant."

"Yes! Do you know what that means?" she asked again.

For a vampire, I was slow processing this, and yet, it all came too fast. A wave of anger built inside me. "Is that what Keeran is for?"

"What? No!" She tsked. "I mean, yes, Morda gave him to me ... hm, yeah, but neither he nor I wanted that. I kept him as my servant so he'd be safe from the other witches."

"But Morda thinks you two are together."

"Yes," she said in a low tone. "And there's more. She cast a spell binding him to me."

A punch to the gut. "What?"

She winced. "It was a surprise. We weren't expecting it, but she did it. We can't be apart for more than a short time."

Rage washed over me like a wave. Before I did or said something stupid, I pushed away from the bed, picked up my pants, and started getting dressed.

Thea stepped right into me. "Drake, I feel only sympathy for him. Keeran has suffered a lot because of the witches, and I pity him. I wanted to help him and it backfired on me." She grabbed my hands and held on tight. "I love you, Drake DuMoir, and only you."

I stared at her, into her beautiful gray eyes. I knew she was telling the truth. I knew her feelings for me were real, and yet I couldn't shake the anger, the jealousy that consumed me alive right now.

"We need to find a way to break that spell."

"Listen to me. Morda wants all our witches pregnant, because she thinks we can produce a witch queen," she said. I had forgotten her coven was the only one without a queen. That and the heart gone ... Thea and her coven had had some hard years before. At least now they had the heart back. "If one of us gives her the witch queen, I'm sure she'll break the spell for me."

"Are you saying you want to give birth to the queen?"

She scoffed. "I don't care, as long as she doesn't kill me when she performs the pregnancy check in a couple of days." She paused and her eyes misted over. "Drake ... you know it's damn hard for a witch to get pregnant, and for the baby to survive the pregnancy and birth, so I confess I never really thought about having children. But, if I'm supposed to have one, then I want her to be yours."

If my dead heart could move, it would be beating out of my chest right now. Ever since becoming a vampire, I hadn't thought about children either. Ninety-nine point nine percent of the male vampires were sterile, so what was the point? But an image flashed in my mind, an image that filled my chest with yearning, with wanting: Thea and I seated on the porch of a white house, hands entwined and smiling at each other, while two beautiful kids laughed and played on the floor around us.

I leaned forward and rested my forehead on hers. "I would love to have kids with you." A soft sob rose to Thea's throat, but she swallowed it. I embraced her. Until another thought came to mind and I froze. "Wait ... if you have a child ... then if it's a girl, she'll be controlled by Morda. If it's a boy ..." I couldn't finish the sentence. We all knew what the witches did to the boys that were born. "I can't allow that."

"Then let's run away," Thea said, resting her cheek on my chest. "Let's run away. We would have to take Keeran with us, but we can work on finding a way to break the bonding spell. Then, we can consider starting a family for real."

It wasn't just Morda and the witches though. Things were looking bleak at DuMoir Castle, and it only got worse by the second. I told Thea about Alex taking the position of lord of the castle, about Thomas's death, and about the monthly feasts.

"He's killing fifty, one hundred innocents per month," I said. "I'm sure he'll start doing these feasts once every fifteen days. Hell, once a week, if we let him." I sighed. "Besides, if I ran, I'm sure he would send his vampires after me. We wouldn't have peace. I don't want to start a family in a world like that."

"I know you're right," she whispered. "I still want to run, but we can't pretend everything is alright and leave Alex in charge. Any ideas on how to bring him down?"

I kissed the top of her head. "Just one. I have a meeting with the alpha of a werewolf pack tomorrow night. I'll try to convince him to join forces with me and attack Alex."

"That would be great," she said, pulling back. "The more you have on your side, the better, right?"

"Right."

"I could talk to Morda," she said. I frowned at her. "She mentioned wanting to meet with me so I can tell her what I learned inside DuMoir Castle. I think she wants intel on how things are, if they are still strong, things like that. If I can make her believe it's a mess in there, that Alex is crazy and people are revolting against him, and things are really unstable, I can convince her to attack the castle too."

"That's brilliant."

"But only if it works."

I kissed the top of her head. "I know you can make it work."

She smiled at me. "You give me too much credit." Her smile faded. "Wait, how did you manage to contact a werewolf pack?"

Hell ...

I ran a hand through my hair. "About that ..." She frowned. Shit. I better blurt it out before it got worse. "Alex threw a new blood slave at me as a spy. Her name is Luana. He has no idea she's a werewolf and wants to skin him alive."

Thea took a large stepped back. "What?" Her gray eyes were brewing up a storm. "You were just giving me a hard time because I have a male servant while you were quiet about your new female blood slave? Are you serious?"

"Thea, it's not like that."

"The hell it isn't," she snapped. "How can you be such a jerk?"

"Yes, I'm a jealous jerk, happy?" I clenched my fists. "Thea, I swear to you, there's nothing between Luana and me. Like you, I don't feel anything for my blood slave. But, like you, I have to pretend to care for her, so Alex will leave me alone." I advanced a step. "Please, believe me."

She matched my stride and retreated. "Why didn't you tell me before?"

"Honestly, because I hadn't even thought about it." It was the truth. Once I had seen Thea in front of me, nothing else mattered. I wanted her and only her. Nothing else. "Thea, we don't have much time left before we both have to go. Please, don't be mad at me. I want to say goodbye to you on good terms."

For a moment, she held on to her stricken pose. Then, her shoulders relaxed and she let out a long breath. "I suppose you're right. But just know I don't like it."

"Then we're even, because I don't like Keeran either."

She made her way back to me. When she was within reach, I snatched her and pulled her against me. I needed to feel her this close before I had to go back.

"So ..." She hooked her arms around my neck. "The plan is to get the witches and the werewolves to attack the castle together?"

"If we can do that, yes, it would be perfect."

"Then let's do it."

I leaned into her and whispered, "I love you," before capturing her mouth with mine.

She melted into me, and it was all I could do not to growl.

We both had to get back, but right now ... right now I wanted her under me one more time.

I pushed her until her legs hit the bed. Slowly, I laid her down and crawled over her.

A twig snapped outside.

I stilled and stared at Thea. "There's someone outside."

11

THEA

With his super vampire speed, Drake got dressed and checked the outside of the cottage.

My mind went into overdrive considering all the possible scenarios: The vampires had followed him. No, the werewolves were checking up on him. Or it was Keeran, coming to tell me Morda was searching for me. He didn't know the location of the cottage though, so it couldn't be him.

I had just finished getting dressed when Drake came back. "It's a witch," he said. "I don't think it would be wise to attack her."

"Attack her? No. Do you think she saw you?"

"No. She seems lost, like she's searching for something."

"Or someone. Maybe she's searching for me." Damn it. So someone had gone to my bedroom after me, and Keeran hadn't fooled them. I hoped he was all right. "Whatever it is, I can handle it. Just go before she finds you here."

"Are you sure?"

I nodded. He was in my space, cupping my face and

claiming my lips. His kiss was soft and quick, and ended way too soon.

"I'll see you soon, my love," he whispered before dashing out with his super speed.

Even knowing he had to leave, we both had to leave, the pain of seeing him gone was almost too much to bear. I placed a hand over my aching heart and sent a silent prayer that Drake and I would be reunited soon.

Now was not the time to be weak. Gathering my courage and strength, I walked onto the porch, ready to face the witch who had found me.

I expected to see Princess Morda or Soraya. Or even Adya or Polina.

But someone else stood on the stone path below the porch steps.

"Ebby?" I stared at her, confused. "What are you doing here?"

"After I yelled at you, I felt bad," she said in a timid voice. "I followed you because I wanted to apologize."

"You f-followed me?" Oh no ...

"I tried. I think you were using magic, because you were going too fast. I couldn't keep up and got lost."

"You were lost? And how did you get here, then?"

She shrugged. "I guess I found my way again."

"H-how long have you been here?"

"Long enough," she whispered.

My heart skipped a beat. "Long enough for ...?"

"To see your vampire leaving the cottage."

My jaw hit the floor. I opened my mouth and closed it a couple of times, trying to come up with some excuse. "I ... what you saw ... I think ... you're mistaken ..."

"It's okay, Thea," she said, her voice a little louder, a little surer. "I won't tell anyone. I promise. If ..." She pressed her lips together.

I didn't dare deny it. If she saw Drake leaving the cottage, even though I was sure he was careful about it, then there was no reason to deny it. "If?" I urged her, wanting to know her price.

"If you help me," she finally said, looking every bit as young and innocent as she was. "You're a hero to the coven now. You have status and a say on things. You can sway the other witches to like me, or at least to stop being mean to me."

I wasn't sure I had the power she thought I had, but it was true that now I was being called for more events and asked my opinions on random things. Maybe I could help her.

"I guess that's doable." I started walking away from the cottage, and Ebby fell into step with me. "How are your spells?"

She snorted. "Pitiful."

"Still weak? Even with the heart back?"

"Actually, I can feel more magic inside me, but I'm having a hard time accessing it."

I frowned. "Maybe we should practice some spells too, see if I can help you access that hidden magic."

She grinned and her face transformed from a little ugly duck to a beautiful swan. "I would like that."

Witches weren't all stunningly beautiful like vampires. During their transformation, vampires became more beautiful, more attractive. It was part of their power. Witches didn't have that kind of beauty, at least not most of us, but we had charm. We knew how to enchant our victims with our magic, and we looked breathtaking while doing it.

In my mind, I could see Ebby flowering, becoming a powerful and beautiful witch.

We walked in the direction of the Silverblood mansion in silence before she asked what I knew she was dying to.

"So," she started, her voice low again. "You and that vampire? Are you two together?"

I didn't answer right away, because honestly, I didn't know what to say. Should I trust her? Could I trust her? I looked at her, pondering. She looked so young and innocent and alone. And I was alone too. I had Keeran, but he had been paired with me by chance. Maybe Ebby could become a friend and ally inside the coven. Maybe she could help me too.

"Yes," I confessed. "Drake and I are together."

"So you lied when you told us what happened at DuMoir Castle?"

I flinched. I hated lying, and yet it seemed it was all I did lately. "Yes, I had to. I couldn't let Morda know I had fallen in love with a vampire."

"What? You're going to continue to sneak off every once in a while to see him?"

Once more, I considered how much to tell her. I decided that if I was going to trust her, then I was going to really trust her. "I won't stay in the Silverblood coven forever."

Her eyes widened and she tripped on her feet. I reached for her, but she recovered her balance before I could touch her. "You, what? How? Why?"

"Drake plans to overthrow Alex and take over the castle," I said. I felt calm about telling her all this. "When he does, I'll leave the coven to be with him."

Her mouth fell open. She snapped it shut. "I ... can I come with you?"

My brows knotted. "What?"

"When you leave to go to DuMoir Castle, can I come with you? As the lady of the castle, you can probably give me some special position at the court, and I could live without having to worry about being mocked by the other witches."

"Do you realize what you're saying?"

"Yes," she said, firmer. "I hate living in the Silverblood coven. I'm kicked around like a piece of trash. I'm tired of it. I would prefer becoming the consort of a beautiful, powerful vampire than continue living like this." She paused. "Besides, you found love with a vampire. Maybe I can too." She shrugged. "What do you say?"

What did I say? I didn't know. "I'll see what I can do," I told her, not really sure about anything. I probably had to talk to Drake about this before promising a position within the castle. I wasn't worried about myself, because if Drake was lord of the castle, no one would dare touch me—I hoped. But having another witch roaming around the castle? I had to make sure she would be okay before saying yes.

I couldn't deny the thought of not being the only witch inside DuMoir Castle was more than pleasant, though. I guess I would have to find a place for Ebby within the castle. Worst case scenario, she could come as my friend and we would deal with the rest later.

It was almost morning when Ebby and I got back to the coven. As most everyone was sleeping, we didn't have much trouble sneaking inside, besides evading a couple of witchguards.

Ebby followed me to my bedroom.

"Keeran?" I called once we were inside. The room was near dark, but I could easily make out no shape on my bed or love seat. My heart sped up. "Keeran?" I rushed around the bedroom, looking for him.

"Keeran is your servant, right?" Ebby asked, glancing around.

"Yes," I said, growing anxious. My bedroom wasn't large enough that he could be hidden in a corner. "Keeran!" I called louder.

"Here," came a faint whisper.

I turned to the bathroom and pushed the door open. I gasped at the sight of Keeran curled on the floor, trembling.

I knelt beside him. "What happened?"

My mind conjured the most horrific images. Morda coming in and torturing him to know where I was. Or Soraya abusing him even though he was now mine, and she would burn if she touched him. Or both.

"Pain," he croaked, his hands splayed over his chest.

I pried his hands away, trying to find his wound. "Where? What happened? Who hurt you?"

"The bond," he hissed. "It's the bond. You were away too long."

By all that was sacred ...

I had known the bond would kick in, but I was hoping it would take longer. And even if it did, I had expected the pain to be more tolerable for the first twenty-four hours. Apparently, Morda didn't play around with her spells.

Guilt consumed me. "I'm so sorry."

"You're here now," he whispered. "It's already better."

And yet, he still wrinkled his nose and clenched his teeth.

Placing my hands on his chest, I called my magic and was stunned when it kicked in faster than it ever had before. I had to really force it to come to life before I retrieved the heart. Now, it was much easier, much faster. Almost as natural as breathing. I focused on healing, on suppressing the pain. I wasn't a witch skilled in healing, and the healing salve wouldn't help with this since it wasn't an open wound, but I could reduce his pain.

A minute later, Keeran stopped shaking. Taking a deep breath, he relaxed and sprawled his large frame on the floor.

"I'm so sorry," I repeated.

"It's okay," he said, looking at me. "We didn't know how potent the spell was."

"What are you feeling now? How can I help?"

"Just a dull pain right now and it's fading." He sat up and groaned. "Or maybe not."

"I can try to take more of your pain," I said, already reaching for his chest.

He gently pushed my hand away. "No, I'll be fine." He started getting up, and I hooked my hand under his arm to help him. "I'm fin—" His words faded when he stood and swayed to the side, dizzy from the pain.

"You're not fine." I put his arm over my shoulders. "You're going to bed right now. Ebby, help me here."

Keeran stared at me with shielded eyes. "Ebby? What are yo—?"

Ebby stepped into the bathroom. "Yes?"

"Help me take him to my bed."

Her brows curled down. "What happened?"

I reminded her of the bond Morda had put on Keeran and me. "We didn't know it would be this strong."

Ebby snorted. "Princess Morda did it. Of course it's strong."

Ebby was smaller than me, but she somehow wrapped her arm around Keeran and helped me take him to my bed.

Groaning some more, Keeran lay down. "I don't want to rest," he said, already closing his eyes. He was fighting pain and exhaustion, but it would only postpone his recovery.

"Just stay there for a while," I snapped, trying to force as much authority into my tone as I could. "That's an order."

He snickered, but didn't say anything.

It didn't take long until his breathing slowed and he fell into a deep sleep. I watched over him for a moment while my mind raced. No matter what I did, where I went, I couldn't leave Keeran behind, not without breaking this bond first. Which meant, if I escaped, if I ran away and went to live with Drake, Keeran would have to come with me. But what if he didn't want to? I couldn't force him to live a life he didn't want.

I added one more item to my long to-do list: Find a way to break my bond with Keeran.

"You care about him," Ebby said as she followed me to the love seat. She sounded surprised.

"I do."

"But ... he's your servant, not your lover. You're not supposed to care about him."

I frowned. "That's so wrong."

"What about Drake? Don't you care about him?"

"When I lived with the vampires, one thing was clear to me: The world isn't black and white. There are several shades of gray. And that applies to feelings too. We don't just love and hate. We can care about a person and not want anything romantic with him." I gestured to her. "Take you, for example. I care about you, and because of that, I want to help you."

She didn't seem convinced. "Why do you care about me? I didn't do anything to make you like me."

In our society, a witch wasn't liked for her kindness, or by who she was on the inside. She was liked, or feared, for her power, for her ranking, for her prowess. Witches didn't have friends; they had allies. As for families, we weren't supposed to love our mothers and grandmothers; we were supposed to revere them. If my grandmother and mother were still alive, I would be crawling in their shadows, worshiping them, and aiming for rewards by committing unspeakable acts.

I was beginning to hate our society.

"I like you because you remind me of myself a couple of years ago," I confessed. "I was alone and weak and afraid." I paused. "But more than that, I like you because you're a young woman trying to break from the mold and be yourself."

She stared at me as if I had grown two heads. "I don't get you. You're too ..." She looked around as if searching for a word in the furniture in my room. "Good. That's the word. You're too good to be a witch."

I shook my head. "To be honest, until a couple of months ago, I didn't see the difference between good or bad. Or evil. We were raised in this society, but no one ever said we were cruel or evil. We just were. We didn't question any of it."

"And living with the vampires changed you? But we were taught they are the true evil in this world."

"It all goes back to nothing being black and white. As there are less bitchy witches here, there are less evil and even some caring vampires there." I paused, feeling like I was being too philosophical for this time of the day. It was probably because I hadn't slept in over twenty-four hours. "Why can't witches be good? Why do we have to be so heartless? To be honest, I want a society where we don't compete against each other, against other covens."

"Then ... what would we do?"

"Live. Laugh. Love. I don't know. Anything but fighting."

"You make it all sound so simple, so ... good." Ebby wrinkled her nose, probably not used to that word.

"It's definitely not simple, but it's what I want."

"It's what you think you'll find with Drake?"

"I'm hoping it is."

One corner of Ebby's lips curled up. "You should be princess instead of Morda. I'm sure you would lead us to a better place."

I scoffed. "Don't let her hear you."

"Oh, no, I would like to keep my head, you know."

I chuckled, taken aback by the fact Ebby was making a joke. She was learning fast. And speaking of learning ... I glanced over my shoulder to my bed. Keeran was sound asleep.

I stood and beckoned to Ebby. "Come on."

"What?" She rose to her feet. "Where are we going?"

I grabbed her shoulders and pushed her back a few feet. "Right here." Then, I rushed to the other side of the room. "Now, we'll practice some basic spells. Are you ready?

A wide smile spread over her lips. "I'm ready!"

We started with the conjuring of flames or balls of light. To my surprise, Ebby even had problems with that. We spent over an hour practicing, and when she was finally able to cast the flames, I moved on to the next step—control over the flames. I showed her how to expand and move the flames and even toss them around, while keeping a leash on them, controlling where they went, what they touched, and the damage they would cause. In the process, she knocked the books off the side table—and Keeran kept on sleeping.

Finally, after so long without sleep, the tiredness got to me in the evening.

"I'll let you rest," she said, heading to the door. She stopped by the door and looked at me, her eyes full of wonder. "Thank you."

"My pleasure." I smiled at her. "You should rest too, because we're practicing again tomorrow."

She nodded, then exited my bedroom.

Alone—except for my sleeping servant—I grabbed a change of clothes and went to the bathroom, where I took a long, hot shower. If I could, I wouldn't wash my skin ever again, just so I could keep Drake's scent on me.

Thinking of him, I went back to my bedroom and glanced at my bed. It was a queen-size and Keeran was occupying half. I could lay down beside him and go to sleep, but for some reason, that didn't feel right.

I settled for the love seat, where I had to curl my legs so I would fit, but it wasn't half bad.

I closed my eyes …

"Thea," a voice called me. I blinked and found Keeran's face above me. "Wake up."

I sat up, realizing I was in my bed. "How …?"

"I woke up and switched with you."

But … I had just closed my eyes. "What time is it?"

"Almost nine at night."

Holy shit, I had slept for a few hours. I already felt a more rested, but I could do that on the love seat. "You're bigger than me," I protested, sitting up. "The love seat will be too uncomfortable for you."

He shook his head. "We can discuss that later. Now you need to get ready."

I rubbed my eyes, trying to shake off the sleep. "Get ready? For what?"

He pressed his lips tight. "A message just came."

I stilled. "A message?"

"Morda is calling the witches for the pregnancy check."

12

I COULD HAVE SLEPT FOR AN ENTIRE WEEK, ESPECIALLY IF I could keep dreaming about Thea. About her soft skin, about her long, blond hair, her red lips, her delicious body. I could also dream about her sweet scent and even sweeter blood.

I sat up with a jerk, my throat parched.

Hell, I needed a drink.

I got dressed in my usual black pants and shirt and went to the dining room. My chest hurt as I halted in front of the table, remembering a crucial detail.

Thomas was gone, and he wouldn't be serving me bottles of blood anymore.

Hell, who cared about the blood? I had lost a dear friend, and the pain it brought would never go away. I knew it wouldn't. It lessened, like the pain of losing my parents and my siblings, but it never went away.

Bristling, I marched into the kitchen and grabbed a bottle of blood. I drank half of it in a single breath. A scent caught my nose and I gulped the rest of the bottle. The strength of the scent increased, and I reached for another bottle, just to be sure, before going back to the living room, where Luana was.

"Want some breakfast?" I asked, raising the bottle.

She wrinkled her nose. "I already ate, thank you very much."

I took my usual seat at the head of dining table and looked out the glass windows. The heavy curtains were drawn and the sun had just set, tinting the sky a dark blue. I wished I could have stayed in the cottage to watch another sunset with Thea, but it was impossible. While we both still had so much to do in our covens, we wouldn't have time to appreciate the sunset or the sunrise together.

"When do you have to report my doings to Alex?" I asked, still looking out.

"Later tonight," she said. "Just before sunrise, actually."

I nodded. "Already know what you're gonna tell him?"

"That you're wallowing in pain and drinking your nights away."

I glanced at her. "Good girl."

She crossed her arms. "Your mood is sourer tonight. I thought after seeing your woman, it would have improved."

"Seeing her for a brief time only reminds me we can't be together yet, and that hurts more than a sword in the gut," I said in a low voice. With her werewolf ears, I was sure Luana had heard me.

"No time for self-pity or crying over open wounds," she snapped. "My alpha wants to meet you tonight, remember?"

I sighed. "Yes, I remember." She was right, of course. Why wallow in my own pain, when I could be acting, making progress in this goddamn quest I chose for myself? The more allies I made, the faster it all would go. I drank another gulp of the blood, then stood. "When are we leaving?"

"Now," she said. "Right now."

Luana didn't waste time. After scolding me for wearing slacks and black shoes to the meeting—how would I run in that?—and realizing I wasn't going to change, she gave up. Together, we exited the castle, pretending we were going for a walk in the garden, even though it wasn't common for vampires to be friendly to their blood slaves. Nobody stopped us, or even looked at us twice. I guess with Luana playing spy, Alex didn't fear anything from me.

Luana and I strolled past the maze, and once out of hearing range, she hid behind a tree, where she took off her clothes, tossed them to me—saying she would need them again when we met her alpha—then transformed into her wolf.

We took off.

When not injured, Luana was almost as fast in her wolf form as I was, which impressed me.

We stopped a few yards from the same hill where I had caught up with her and found out her secret a couple of nights ago. She bit down, taking her clothes from me, and disappeared behind some bushes. A minute later, Luana emerged wearing black leggings and long white blouse—and barefoot. Because of the added volume, we had opted for leaving her shoes behind.

"Where are they?" I asked, glancing up the hill. I didn't see anyone, and when I used my senses to try to find them, I could only hear and smell the woods.

A sly grin spread over her lips. "They will show up when we get to the top." She walked past me. "Come on."

Wary, I followed her up the hill. I thought I could trust her—I wanted to trust her—but I was dealing with werewolves. My relationship with these creatures had always been strenuous.

"What now?" I asked once we reached the top. I glanced around, but didn't see anything.

"Wait," she whispered.

A minute passed.

Then another.

And one more.

I opened my mouth to ask her if she was playing me, when I sensed them. Their presence, their scent, their heat, their power ... I couldn't be sure, but there were a lot of werewolves approaching us.

"How many dog guards does your alpha need?" I asked, trying to lighten the mood. I didn't like being cornered by so many supernaturals.

"Enough to deal with a powerful vampire, if needed," she said.

Finally, they emerged from the woods and marched up the hill like a wave of pure prowess. They were all in their human form, and most of them were naked. Their alpha, though, was easily recognizable by the leather pants and loose shirt. His hair was long and whipping in the gentle breeze.

He halted a good six feet from me, flanked by two men, who I assumed were his two betas.

Luana lowered her head, in respect to her alpha, then gestured to him. "Prince Drake, this is Ulric, the alpha of the Dark Vale pack."

"Well, well," Uric said, smiling wide. His canines were elongated and sharp, almost like fangs. "Prince Drake of DuMoir Castle requested a meeting. I wonder why?"

I frowned at Luana before returning my gaze to the alpha. "I thought Luana had explained."

"Oh, she did," he said. It hadn't escaped me that he hadn't glanced at her once since arriving, not even when she introduced me to him. "But I would love to hear everything from your own mouth."

I wasn't liking this. Ulric looked like an arrogant ass who thought too highly of himself—he reminded me of Alex. However, I knew from experience not all arrogant asses were evil like Alex was.

And I wasn't here to make friends. I needed allies. All we had to do was draw a good plan and follow through with it.

I summoned my best political voice and started, "I know werewolves and vampires have always been enemies, but we can change that." Ulric didn't seem amused by my words. I went on. "Alex is in charge of DuMoir Castle right now, and he's changing all the rules Lord Reynard imposed."

"You say that as if Lord Reynard had been generous to us," the man on Ulric's right said. One of his betas.

"Rollin," Ulric snapped. "Let the vampire plead his case."

They were having fun with this, and I didn't like it. I suppressed a growl. "All Lord Reynard did was to ensure peace between all supernaturals. He tried to avoid war at all costs."

"By oppressing our race," Rollin said, his fists clenched. "We heard about your little mission a month or so ago. You killed the alpha, betas, and the entire inner circle of a strong pack in northern Canada."

It had been my last mission before Lord Reynard had been killed. I had spent thirteen days fighting nonstop. It had exhausted me, but I had been satisfied with the results.

"I did what I had to do to maintain peace," I snarled.

"That pack wanted to reveal our secret to the world. They wanted to take over the humans and change everything."

"What's so bad about that?" the wolf asked.

I shook my head. "First, the humans would freak out. Second, it would mean another world war. Their numbers are way larger than ours. They might not have our abilities, but they do have powerful weapons that can kill us."

"I agree with the vampire on this," Ulric said, surprising me. "As much as I would like more liberty, we are better off if our existence is unknown."

I sighed in relief. Now I knew how to play his game. "Alex is plotting against the closest werewolf packs and witch covens. He wants to take over the lands around the castle, and he plans on killing every one of you." That was a lie. I had no idea what Alex was plotting now since I had no access to his meetings, but I was sure it couldn't be good. "He wants to be the supreme lord of all supernaturals." The betas growled, while a cool mask fell over the alpha's rough face. I could win this. "If you help me overthrow Alex, I can promise you more freedom. We can draw a peace treaty that will ensure you keep your lands. In fact, I can give you more lands." That wasn't a lie. Werewolves need more land to run the way they liked. Vampires only needed a little land to hunt. I could donate a few acres of the vast DuMoir estate to them.

"What makes you so sure we can win?" Ulric asked.

"Alex doesn't have the support of all the vampires. Some hate him as much as I do. I'm sure we can get a handful of strong vampires on our side." I paused for effect, knowing my next words could make or break the deal. "I'm also working with the Silverblood coven."

"What?" Rollin asked. "Why?"

"That doesn't matter." I wouldn't explain my relationship with Thea to them. "What matters is that when we attack, the Silverblood witches will help us." I hoped Thea was able to convince Princess Morda. "And we can then easily overthrow Alex and take over the castle."

Ulric's brows slammed down and he turned around, to his betas. The three of them talked in hushed whispers, and I only caught a few words they uttered.

Jealous. War. Witches. Damned. Hell. Fuck it. A big problem. Useful ally. More lands. Trust.

The tension inside me piled up during the ten minutes the three talked.

"How long does this usually take?" I asked Luana in a low tone.

"It depends on how important the matter is," she replied. "And this one is pretty important."

Hell ...

Another ten minutes passed, until finally Ulric turned to me with a wide smile.

He extended his hand toward me, and I couldn't help but noticed his fingers had transformed into claws. "We have a deal."

Relief rushed through me. I took his hand and shook it tight. "Great."

We discussed a couple more details, like when to meet next, how to send messages back and forth, and when they should be ready to attack—hopefully we would meet again when it was time for the battle. If we needed to send messages, he would send a wolf to track down Luana, and I would send Luana. As for being ready to attack, I told them to give me a few days then be ready regardless. The moment I heard from Thea, we would go for it.

At the end of the meeting, Ulric and I shook hands again.

"Hope to hear from you soon," Ulric said.

"You will."

Finally, after an hour here, the alpha landed his eyes on Luana. "May I have a word with my wolf?" he asked, though he could have ordered it.

"Sure." I stepped back, giving her space.

Head lowered, Luana marched past me and followed Ulric down the hill, with the betas close behind them. The other fifty or so wolves stayed positioned around the hilltop, all watching me.

What a distrustful bunch.

This time, I couldn't hear any exchanged words, but the fact that Luana didn't look in her alpha's eyes once told me volumes.

After lowering her head even more to him, she spun on her dirty heels and scurried to me.

"Let's go," she uttered, pushing past me.

I frowned, wanting to ask what was wrong. But I held my tongue, because she didn't seem open to talk to me, and because if her alpha asked for secrecy, she was expected to keep it. I could get her in trouble.

I caught up with her and we returned to the castle. My chest was lighter, though, as it seemed I was a step closer to defeating Alex and taking back the castle.

13

———————

THEA

MY HANDS TREMBLED AS I RUSHED TO THE MAIN HALL. I HAD told Keeran to stay behind, but he said he wanted to be there, just in case.

In case of what? As if he could protect me if something happened.

Twice, fear overcame me, and I stopped in the middle of the hallway, considering running. Right now. Just grab Keeran's hand and run. We couldn't go to DuMoir Castle right now, and I had no idea how Drake's dealings with the werewolves were going, so I couldn't ask refuge from them either.

Keeran and I could hide in the cottage for now, until Drake was able to meet us and came up with a solution. Because there had to be another way, right?

"Thea," Keeran whispered from behind me the third time I stopped. "We have to go, or you'll be late."

"Late for what?" I snapped. "My death?"

Because surely, I wasn't pregnant after sleeping with Drake only a few times. Especially because he was a vampire. If he had been human, I would be more hopeful.

I still wasn't sure about bringing a child into this crazy, violent world.

"Princess Morda might make an exception for the current hero," he said. "But if you don't show up, then she'll hunt you down."

He was right.

I held on to the hero card, ready to play it the moment she checked me and found out I wasn't pregnant.

In the main hall, Morda stood in front of her chair, watching with eagle eyes as the witches entered the room and lined up in several rows. Keeran stayed with the other servants by the walls and I rushed forward. I found a place right in the middle, and Ebby stood beside me.

"How are you holding up?" I asked her. She looked as nervous as I felt.

"Not well," she whispered. "I ... I haven't t slept with a servant lately."

My eyes widened. "But ... she'll find out. What are you—?"

"It seems you're all here." Princess Morda's voice boomed through the hall. The last time I checked, we were over two hundred witches. Were all of us here? I glanced around and gasped at the crowded room. "Stay in your places. I'll go around and use my magic to detect any pregnancies."

When Morda moved to the first line of witches, the tension in the room was palpable. She placed her hand on the stomach of the first. Three seconds later, she grinned. "Well done. You're pregnant."

The witch's shoulders dropped in relief.

I could see the second witch in line shaking from where I stood. Morda rested her hand on her stomach. This time, it took five seconds, but finally Morda announced, "You're not pregnant yet, but I can sense male seeds inside you. Well done."

I thought the young witch would fall to the ground when Morda moved to the next witch.

Wait ... Morda could sense the man's sperm inside a witch? We didn't have to be pregnant yet?

The hope flaring inside me was short-lived.

Drake was a vampire and chances were he was sterile, like the vast majority. There would be no sperm inside me.

Holy ...

My hands trembled more with each passing minute, and I only noticed I had started fidgeting with the skirt of my gown when Ebby slapped my hand, getting my attention.

To stop the nervous habit, I put my arms behind my back and entwined my fingers together. Tight.

Then Morda was on the line before mine, checking the witch right in front of me. So far, all the witches had passed the check.

"I can't sense a baby or a man's seed inside you," Morda said, her voice rising with a biting edge. "Carlyn, you're sentenced to the bloodbone ritual."

I gasped.

Two witchguards appeared beside a wide-eyed Carlyn and took her by the arms. They started carrying her away from the other witches, when Myrna, another witch who had already passed the test jumped out.

"No!" A black flame appeared in her hand, and she threw it at Morda.

Morda didn't even blink. She swept her arm to the side and the flame faded. Then she pointed a finger at Myrna.

The crack of several bones breaking echoed through the hall.

Her body fell to the floor.

Horror filled me.

"No!" Carlyn yelled, finally waking up from her shock. She thrashed against the witchguards. "Myrna, my love. No!"

Whispers began somewhere in the back and spread.

"They were lovers."

"Carlyn refused to lie with a man."

"But Myrna did it for them."

"And now both will pay."

My heart sank.

Without ceremony, Morda walked to the end of the hall. The two larger glass doors opened inward, and she went outside, followed by the witchguards and a screaming Carlyn.

"All of you, move, now," Soraya snapped.

Falling out of formation, the other witches and I rushed to the large stone patio outside and gathered in a circle around Morda and Carlyn.

With a wave of Morda's hands, two stone pillars jutted from the ground. The witchguards chained Carlyn to the pillars, then stepped back, returning the show to Morda.

"Pay attention," Morda said, her voice ringing in our ears.

A long hunting knife appeared in her hand and she began. Morda dragged the knife from Carlyn's collarbone to her pelvis. At first, Carlyn screamed and jerked, but when Morda repeated the gestured on her arms—from the shoulders to her palms—Carlyn went silent.

I turned my face away.

I could hear the blade as Morda continued her cruel work, cutting Carlyn open while keeping her conscious with magic. I didn't need to look to know what happened next. We all had heard the stories, the tales. Although, I had never seen it, had never heard the chilling screams, then the terrifying silence.

Next, Morda pulled out Carlyn's organs one by one. She put them in a pile and set them on fire. Then, it was time for the bones. Morda ripped out Carlyn's bones. With magic, she twisted the bones until they snapped.

Only after that was done did Morda drop the magic keeping her victim alive.

Carlyn whimpered one more time.

The chain loosened and her limp body fell to the ground.

I forced myself to look up as Morda, with blood on her hands, arms, gown, and face, turned and looked at us. "Carlyn and Myrna were lovers. I don't care as long as they followed my orders. Witches who aren't performing their duties to the coven will be considered traitors, and treachery will not be tolerated." She wiped her hands on her gown, but I wasn't sure which one was more bloodied. "That's enough of a show for tonight. Those of you whom I haven't checked yet tonight, consider yourselves lucky. You have a couple more days to try again." She waved her bloody hands. "Now go."

The witches around me hurried inside the mansion as if afraid that, if Morda caught them, they would be next.

But I couldn't move. I couldn't breathe.

Two witches had died here, two witches who loved each other, and despite the gruesome punishment, everyone would be returning to their normal lives in a matter of minutes.

By all that was scared, when did we become so cruel, so heartless?

Ebby caught my arm and tugged. "Come before Morda notices you."

What if she did? What would she do? Perform the blood-bone ritual on me because I was appalled?

I wanted to see her try.

I clenched my fists and felt the magic rushing through my veins.

"Thea," Keeran muttered somewhere behind me. "Please, let's go."

What would happen to Keeran if I died? Would the bond break or kill him too? I let out a long breath. I couldn't be this careless.

Reality crashed over me like a waterfall. I inhaled sharply.

What was I doing? I was weak, even with the heart's magic around. I couldn't take Morda by myself.

"Yes, let's go," I whispered, finally turning and following Keeran and Ebby back into the mansion.

Morda wasn't kidding. If I was caught looking the wrong way, I could also end up a victim of the bloodbone ritual.

There was too much to do to be caught and killed just yet.

14

DRAKE

Since coming back from the meeting with the wolves a week ago, I had been on edge. More than usual.

Alex kept me in the dark, and princes I had once considered allies—Cain, Phelps, and Gray, especially—wouldn't tell me anything out of fear of the new lord of the castle. I had thought about contacting them and asking them for their allegiance, but since they were avoiding me now, I decided to wait. Luana, who was sound asleep in her bedroom now, didn't tell me why she wouldn't look at her alpha and what he had said to her before we came back, even though I had brought the subject up twice now. Thea hadn't sent me messages to meet her, or to let me know she was all right. I hated that.

I stopped pacing the living room and reached for the bottle of blood on the coffee table. It was empty, damn it.

A deep, dull tug started inside my chest. I knew this tug. I had felt it before. It was Thea. It was my longing, my feelings for her. It was the crazy bond between us.

I had to see her.

Right now.

I had no idea how I would reach her inside her coven, but I had to try.

Determined, I turned to the door.

I halted when a murky, shadow figure appeared in front of me.

The hair on my arms stood on end and I took a step back.

What magic was this?

"My Prince," a faint voice said.

I frowned. Where had I heard this voice before?

The murky figure gained the shape of a person. A young man.

Realization downed on me right before his face came into focus. "Thomas!"

He bowed his head to me. "Hello, my Prince."

I stared at him, mouth hanging open. "A ghost? How …?"

"I've been trying to contact you for a few days now, my Prince, but it wasn't easy to get a hold of this form. Being a ghost is harder than it looks."

Though I knew ghosts existed, I had never seen one before. "But I thought … why are you stuck here?"

"It seems I have unfinished business," Thomas said. The shock of seeing him as a whitish, semitransparent form still hadn't passed. "I confess that when I was alive, something bothered me, and I think once I solve it, I'll be allowed to move on."

"And what is that?" If there was anything I could do to help him, I would.

"I need to find out who killed my parents," he said. If I had a beating heart, it would have stopped. "A vampire killed my parents that night, my Prince, and I need to find out who it was. Once I find out, I'll be able to go on. I'll be able to be reunited with my family. Since you're the one who saved me, I'm hoping you will help me find out who killed my parents."

"Thomas …"

"I know, my Prince. I know you're busy dealing with Alex, and nothing would please me more at the moment than seeing you take him down. It would feel like revenge, and I'm sure I would have some peace with that, too."

"Yes, Alex …"

"Now that I seem to have more control of my form, I vow to be a faithful servant. I'll spy on Alex and the other princes for you and find out anything that can be used against them."

I clenched my teeth. "That would be good," I muttered.

"I'm running out of strength to hold on to this form, my Prince," Thomas said, as if he had been a ghost for decades and knew how it all worked. "I'll lurk around Alex and tell you all I find out once I'm able to contact you again."

"Yes, but—"

Thomas's ghost blurred and faded like smoke.

I stared at the spot where he had been a moment ago, still shaken.

I plopped on the couch as guilt and shame rushed through me.

I didn't know how Alex was conducting the feast now, but before it was rare that entire families were invited to the castle. Usually, it was one person per family. But an eight-year-old Thomas had come with his parents.

That night, I had had an argument with Alex that left me seeing red. Despite my will to gain control over my rage, I snapped. Fury took hold of me, but as I was about to take it out on Alex, I smelled the blood coming from the ballroom.

The warm, sweet blood.

I had no control. I jumped off the balcony and took the first human who crossed my path.

I only stopped when I tripped over a young boy curled in a ball in the middle of the ballroom. So small, he had been missed by Dorian and Albert, who loved to feed on kids. I was about to walk away when arms wrapped around my legs.

"Please, help me," the boy said, burying his head on my knees.

It broke me.

It all broke me.

The control snapped into place along with the same guilt and shame I still felt now.

I carried the boy away from the ballroom and treated him like a son, like a brother, for two years.

Until he was killed last week by a crazy vampire.

Only I could end Thomas's curse and send him away, but how could I tell him that I had been the one who killed his parents?

15

THEA

EBBY KICKED A ROCK, SENDING IT STRAIGHT INTO THE LAKE. "I can't do this."

"You have to focus," I told her for the thousandth time.

"Easier said than done," she mumbled.

We had been at the edge of the lake on the coven's grounds for the last couple of hours, practicing magic. A week had passed since the first pregnancy check and the bloodbone ritual, and I still couldn't sleep.

Thankfully, there had been no more pregnancy checks, though Morda kept saying it was coming, and we were given a respite. But the tension inside the mansion was palpable. It made me sick to see servants being ordered from bedroom to bedroom.

Concerned about when Morda would perform pregnancy tests again, I cast a simple cloaking spell on Keeran and sent him to deliver a message to Drake twice—and twice he couldn't get near the castle. Vampires patrolled the estate, and a few werewolves ran through the woods. The cloaking spell hid Keeran's scent too, but the vampires weren't fools.

Witches and their magic were one of their many enemies. Apparently, there were now new wards preventing anyone with magic from getting too close.

Trying to speed things up, I had requested a meeting with Morda. I had no idea what I would tell her yet, but somehow I had to convince her to attack DuMoir Castle. However, she still hadn't granted me the honor of meeting with her.

Meanwhile, Ebby, Keeran, and I liked to spend our days outside. We talked about escaping and the future, and we practiced magic.

"I know," I told her, feeling like a hypocrite. I asked her to focus when even I couldn't do it.

My nerves were shot between not seeing Drake, fearing Morda's wrath, and planning to run away.

"Can we take a break, please?" Ebby asked. She didn't wait for me to answer. Instead, she sat down beside Keeran under the shade of a tree.

I inhaled deeply and looked to the blue sky. I loved Drake and would gladly adapt to his night schedule, but I couldn't lie. I had missed the daylight. Nothing like the warmth of the sun kissing my skin to make me feel reinvigorated. If I closed my eyes and conjured an image of Drake and me hiding in the cottage forever, I could almost believe it.

"What are you thinking?" Keeran asked.

During this last week, he had changed a lot. At least when alone with Ebby and me. He was becoming confident and speaking freely, like a real friend. I also thought he was less afraid, but I knew he still feared one thing above all others. Because of the damned bond, I couldn't run away without him, but he hadn't mustered the courage to escape Morda's clutches. Keeran feared her punishments.

We all did.

Though I researched and tried the spells I knew, I still hadn't found a way to break the bond. For now, Keeran was tied to me as a fish was tied to the water.

I approached them, but remained in the sun. "About life after this ..."

Ebby tilted her head. "This what?"

"This ..." I gestured toward the mansion in the distance. From here, it looked like a sprawling stone castle—erected to last several millennia. "This place, this rule, this torture. We're afraid of our own shadows here. I hate it."

"Are you really sure your plan will work?" Ebby asked.

I crouched down. "I barely have a plan. Right now, I have a wish list."

"But we're working on a plan, right?"

"Yes. Hopefully, we'll find one soon." I hoped. We couldn't live like this much longer. It wasn't fair. It wasn't right.

And yet, it was the only way the witches knew.

If only I could show them a different way ...

They would never hear me. If they heard me, they would laugh in my face, then kill me outright for having such thoughts.

No, that wasn't part of the plan. We had to be smart about this.

A loud crash came from the mansion and I stood, suddenly on alert.

"What was that?" Ebby asked, coming to my side.

Screams rang through the air.

"I don't know." I stepped forward, but was stopped by a firm grip on my wrist. "What is it?"

Another crash.

"Something is wrong," Keeran said, holding me back. "Don't go."

"I have to find out what's going on," I told him, prying his fingers from my arm. "Stay here and hide."

He lowered his head as if I had given him an order. That hadn't been my intention. I was merely suggesting . As a human servant, he didn't know how to fight and he didn't possess any magic to help us, so it was better if he stayed out of the way.

"Let's go," Ebby said, sprinting toward the mansion.

I went after her.

The loud bangs and screams increased in volume and frequency the closer we got to the mansion. Flashes of light shone past the windows.

"What's going on?" Ebby whispered.

I put my arm in front of her and slowed. "I don't like this. Be careful."

She nodded.

Side by side, we crept up to one of the many doors of the mansion. We spied inside. My breath caught.

Witches ran down the hallway beyond the door, screams echoed through the walls, and magic flew without direction. But there weren't only Silverblood witches. There were plenty of faces I had never seen before, which meant there was another coven here.

We were under attack.

"By all that is sacred," Ebby muttered, her face white.

No time to be scared. I channeled my magic and it answered, waking up from its slumber and filling my veins. "Let's go." I stepped into the mansion, and half a second later had to cast a shield to protect us from the incoming spells. My shield was weak and broke after a dozen or so spells bounced off it. I pulled Ebby to hide behind a column jutting out of the wall. "It seems some witches are throwing spells at random, hoping to hit the enemy. Be careful."

A witch from our coven flew past us and slammed into the wall on the other side of the hallway. She slumped to the floor.

"I'll help her," Ebby said. Ducking the incoming magic, she rushed to the fallen witch and dragged her inside a room. If they were smart, they would hide inside, barricade the door, and pray this was over quick.

I wanted to find out what was going on, what coven it was, and where they had come from. Had there been any warnings or signs?

Fighting my way through the hallways, I rushed to the main hall.

As I expected, Morda, Soraya, the inner circle, and a crap load of witchguards were all there.

What I didn't expect was to find Sarah, the Witch Queen of the Blackmarsh coven, standing in the middle of the room as if she owned the place.

Quiet as a mouse, I slipped in and plastered myself along the drawn curtains of a window.

"I heard some interesting rumors," Queen Sarah said, apparently not one bit concerned that she was surrounded by over fifty witches. And she looked spectacular, to be honest. Her black dress was simple and elegant, with a tight bodice and slits in the front, revealing black leather pants underneath. Her long, silver hair was tied in a thick braid that fell down her back, to her knees. And a black crown of twisted thorns sat atop of her head. "Besides not having a witch queen, I've been hearing you lost the heart of the coven to vampires a while back, dear Princess Morda."

Morda didn't seem affected. She clamped her hands in

front of her and smiled at Queen Sarah. "Interesting rumors. But I'm glad to inform you I sent a witch to recover the heart."

"There are more rumors," Queen Sarah continued. "That the witch you sent to recover the heart was caught by the vampires. She's their blood slave now and can't finish her mission." The queen leaned forward and cupped a hand around her mouth as if she were going to tell a secret. "I also heard she enjoyed becoming a blood slave and has no intention of coming back. She has sided with the vampires now."

My stomach dropped.

Where did she hear that? Her info wasn't wrong, but it was incomplete.

Worried, I watched Morda for her reaction.

"Well, that's where your rumors went wrong," Morda said, smiling. "My witch was caught, but she already had the heart in her hands. She fought and won. The heart is safe now."

Queen Sarah tilted her head. "Is that so? I would like you to prove it." She threw her hand, and black sparks flew from her palm straight to Morda.

Even though she was much weaker than a queen, Princess Morda was no fool. She had been ready for the assault. The moment Queen Sarah moved, Morda moved too.

But I stopped paying attention to their fight as Queen Sarah's words sank in. The rumor ... she had lied about it. She probably knew I had made it back with the heart. But since it had been taken once, it could be easily taken twice. She had been playing Morda, checking if we really had the coven's heart back.

Because she would steal it.

My breath caught.

I had to get to the heart. I had to protect it, to save it, before it was too late.

I glanced at the fight going on in the middle of the room as I crept to the door. Even though she was one against dozens, Queen Sarah was kicking everyone's butt. Only Morda seemed to be a challenge for her, but even then, I doubted our princess would be able to hold on much longer.

I thought about stepping forward and helping, but what difference would that make? I wasn't strong. I would only die faster. No, I had to get to the heart and keep it safe. Then maybe, just maybe, my coven would have a chance to survive.

With everyone distracted with the fight, slipping out of the main hall wasn't hard. I ran past fallen witches, from both the Silverblood and the Blackmarsh covens. My heart tugged with guilt. I wanted to stop and help my coven, but I couldn't. Not now.

Saving the heart was more important.

I turned into the hallway leading to the tower and my steps faltered. At the end of the corridor, the witchguards who were supposed to be guarding the door were sprawled on the floor, and the thick door was open.

Damn it.

Despair pushed me and I ran into the tower. I glanced up the winding stairs. I couldn't see the second door from here, but I could see three witches halfway to the top.

Gritting my teeth, I started up the stairs and threw a blue flame at them. It bounced off the stone steps, as I thought it would, but at least I had gotten their attention.

"Why you ...?" the white-haired witch snarled. She threw a spell at me, but I dodged it by hiding under the stairs.

I heard their footsteps, coming down the steps, and got ready.

I jumped at them before they could jump at me, and threw a wave of magic at them. They stumbled, and two of them fell on the stones steps. The white-haired witch threw a spell at me, but I conjured a shield in front of myself. But then the other two witches were up and flinging their magic at me. My shield blinked and broke.

I gasped a moment before three black bolts hit me in the chest and flung me back. I hit the stone wall hard, and the air rushed out of my lungs. They held me up with their magic, pushing me against the wall, crushing my body and soon my bones. The air kept failing me, and I knew if I didn't break from this spell soon, I would die—either crushed to pieces or by suffocation.

With her hand up, holding the spell in place, the white-haired witch stepped closer and smiled at me. "I heard about you. The young witch who went into the vampire coven for a suicide mission, but who made it back in one piece—and with the coven's heart." Her dark eyes ran the length of me, sizing me up. "Not so tough now, are you?"

This bitch ...

A roar burst from my chest as I fought against their spell. Pain prickled every inch of my body, of my skin, but I fought against it. I felt like it was being ripped out of me, but I pushed through the pain and reached for her extended arm.

"You talk too much," I rasped, closing my hand around her wrist and pulling her closer. Meanwhile, with my other hand, I pulled Drake's dagger from its strap around my hips.

The witch's eyes widened when I pierced the dagger deep into her gut.

She stumbled forward and the magic holding me faded.

The other two stared at me, too shocked to react. I didn't hesitate. I swept my arm in a wide arc, and my magic rushed out in a powerful wave. The two witches flew backward, hit the wall, and continued rolling down the steps.

I hurried up the rest of the stairs, taking the steps two at a time. Hopefully, the witches would be unconscious for a while. If they weren't, I would deal with them. Right now, I had to make sure the heart was okay.

My heart failed when I reached the top and found the enchanted door pushed down on the floor and a witch standing on it.

Lynne, Queen Sarah's right hand.

"If it isn't Thea, the Silverblood hero," she said, grinning at me. Her smile reminded me of Morda's when she was plotting her wicked and evil plans, but for some reason, while I feared Morda, I was terrified of Lynne. The things I heard she could do ... I shuddered. "I confess I was expecting it to be harder to get to your coven's heart. I mean, you already lost it once. Why make it so easy to lose it twice?"

In the back of my mind, I was shocked too. I thought Morda would have cast five hundred thousand ancient spells around the tower and placed another five hundred witchguards on the outside to make sure it was never stolen again. I wanted to blame it on the fact that we were attacked without warning or expectation. But even so, Morda should have been smarter about it. But that was a matter for another day. Right now, I had to think of a way I could survive Lynne and get to the heart before she did.

"Who said it's not a trap?" I lied, forcing my voice to remain firm, when in truth I was shaking on the inside.

Lynne narrowed her eyes at me. "Let's see how much of a hero you are." She threw black sparks at me.

I barely had time to move and hide behind the wall. The sparks exploded on the other side of the tower, singeing the stones black.

As much as I liked the safety of the thick stone wall

between us, Lynne was inside the room with the heart while I was out here.

Closing my eyes, I channeled my magic. It answered fast and filled me up. Then, I stepped under the doorway and pushed my hands out, letting it all go. I screamed, not caring about how much it took from me, as long as I won.

But Lynne was strong. While the other three witches would have flown across the room, Lynne only slid backward a few feet as she fought against my power.

I kept my focus on the magic, on Lynne, but I accessed the room. Round and not as large as I thought it would be. Right in the middle, three stone steps rose to form a platform, and in the middle of the platform, a stone pedestal supported a round, silver marble basin. And inside the basin, I could see the heart, beating in a steady rhythm.

The heart of the first witch of my coven. The powerful object that wielded our magic. The only thing, besides a witch queen, that could keep us alive and well.

The heart had to be saved.

With every ounce of strength I had left, I pushed more of my magic at Lynne. And she pushed against it.

She was more powerful than I was, and she proved that when, still fighting against my magic, she conjured a black bolt and flung it at me—right at my chest.

I took a step back and waved my arm down, sending my magic out to meet the bolt, which faded a second later. But in the process, I had let go of the magic holding Lynne, and she wasn't the forgiving kind.

She threw another bolt at me. And another. And another.

I sidestepped, cut through a few more, and even ran out of the way of some more. After a minute or two, I realized what she was doing. Lynne was getting me tired, by dodging and running all around. The more tired I was, the harder it would be to fight back. After she was doing playing with me, I wouldn't have any energy left to protect the heart.

Needing a second to think, I knelt and conjured a thick shield in front of myself. The bolts increased in frequency, hitting my shield with loud booms and leaving tiny cracks behind.

I didn't know what to do. Thinking wouldn't save me now, not when Lynne was so much stronger than I was. It was a miracle I had lasted this long already.

But I wouldn't go down without giving all of me.

I let out a yell and channeled the magic from deep in my core. I let a big blue flame out toward Lynne.

She conjured a shield half a second before it reached her. The flames broke through her shield and she stumbled back with the impact.

She groaned. "You're playing with my patience."

Lynne opened her arms wide and then closed them, her hands twisted into claws. Pure magic enveloped me, like a heavy blanket wrapped around me.

I jerked against it as it crushed me and lifted me from the floor, but I could barely move my arms. Her eyes on me, Lynne took three deliberate steps toward the pedestal.

No, no, no ...

Like I had done before, I fought against the magic's hold and reached for the dagger at my hip. I would throw it at her, right at her heart. I didn't have the best aim for that, but maybe if I used the rest of my magic to guide the dagger, I could do it. I could kill her from across the room.

But Lynne saw the moment I pulled it out. She waved her hand at me, and my own twisted in an awkward way. I yelled as pain ran up my arm and the dagger fell to the ground.

"I have to say," Lynne said, taking another step toward the heart. "I'm impressed. I see now how you survived the vampire coven. You are resilient and stubborn. Good qualities in a witch. It's a shame you belong to a rival coven."

She turned her back to me and reached for the heart.

Something inside me snapped.

I roared.

The magic around me faded.

I ran toward the heart.

Lynne stared at me with wide eyes as I took the heart in my hand before she did.

Power filled my veins and rushed like blood through me. I felt replenished. I felt strong. I felt invincible.

I raised my free arm, palm out, and a bright blue light emanated from it, rushing out like ripples in the water.

Lynne screamed.

A moment later, there was nothing but a pile of dust on the stone floor.

Heart hammering, I stared at it.

Just like in the woods when Alex's vampires had found me.

I shifted my gaze to the beating heart in my hand. It was the heart. It was its power. I extended my hand, intent on dropping it in the basin again, but a thought stopped me. I could stay here and protect it, or I could take it down and use it to win this battle.

A sliver of guilt and shame snaked inside my chest—after all, I shouldn't be touching the heart—but I could feel guilty and shameful later. Right now, I had a coven to save.

I hid the heart under the skirt of my gown and ran down the stairs.

When I got back into the main hall, I paused.

There were bodies on the floor—if they were dead or alive, I didn't know—but Morda, Soraya, and a handful of witches from our coven still fought Queen Sarah, who didn't seem tired at all.

I moved toward the fight as Queen Sarah shot hundreds of black sparks toward Morda and the other witches. Soraya, who was actually bleeding from her shoulder, cast a shield in front of them. The sparks hit the shield like a round of bullets, and the shield broke.

Queen Sarah cackled, probably sensing she was close to finishing this.

Oh no, she wouldn't.

I jumped in front of Morda and faced the queen. "Not today," I rasped.

Like it had done twice now, the heart acted alone. Its power coursed through me, lifting my hands toward Queen Sarah, and its magic flew out my palms. It traveled in an arc toward the Queen.

Her face paled and a thick shield rose in front of her.

My magic broke through her shield, like it had ripped through paper, and exploded into her.

Queen Sarah skidded back until she slumped into the wall across the room. She looked down at her arm. Red welts covered her once smooth skin.

"You'll pay for this," she snarled.

The magic flowed through me once more, and I was ready to hit her again. But, to my surprise, Queen Sarah ran.

The Queen of the Blackmarsh ran.

Crickets could be heard inside the main hall.

I turned to Morda. "Are you okay?"

She stared at me with wide eyes. I had never seen such unguarded expression from her before.

Slowly, she approached me. "How ... how did you do that?"

I shrugged. "I don't know," I lied. "I feel stronger since having the heart back." Or since using the heart. If she found out I touched the heart, that the heart was now in my pocket, she would kill me on the spot.

She placed her hands on my shoulders. "I'm proud of you." She squeezed hard then turned around and looked at the damage in the room. Now that the battle was over, I realized most of the bodies on the floor weren't dead witches. They were simply too hurt to get up or fainted, but not dead.

"Is it over?" Polina asked, crawling toward us.

Vera appeared by her side and both of them got up. "I think so."

A scream came from outside.

"Soraya!" Morda said, her voice in its usual commanding tone. "Take a few witchguards with you and check the rest of the mansion. Make sure all the Blackmarsh are either dead or gone."

"Yes, my Princess." Soraya bowed her head, and then marched out of the main hall.

Morda looked at me again, and I felt like hiding behind a wall. "What is it, my Princess?" Had she figured it out? By all that was sacred, if she figured it out ...

"We've won," she said, her eyes darkening. "We have won this battle. We almost crushed the Blackmarsh coven, one of the most powerful witch covens out there. By all that was sacred, you were able to burn their Queen." She nodded once. "Now is the time."

"For what, my Princess?"

"To attack. We should attack the other covens now."

"But ..." I had no idea what to say to her. That wasn't part of the plan. Attack other witches? No, no. We had to attack the vampires, damn it.

"We'll talk about this later," she said, looking around. "Now we have work to do. Clean up the mansion and heal the wounded. Go help out." She waved me off.

I lowered my head in a bow. "Yes, my Princess."

My breathing shallow, I walked out of the main hall, as if I was ready to help the other witches.

I had already helped, more than I probably should have.

My head spun with too many thoughts. I had so much to think about, to decide, but I couldn't do it alone.

Determined, I went back to the tower and pulled the heart from under my dress. Its beat sped up once it was in my hand. What was it? Why did I feel so drawn and close to the heart? Shaking my head, I rested the heart back in its place.

I ignored the pile of dust on the floor, and using the little magic I had left, I pulled the door up and against the door-jamb. I would tell Morda its enchantment was gone later—or hopefully she would notice it without me uttering a word.

A long sigh escaped my lips.

Now that that was done, I went outside to find Keeran.

He saw me coming toward the servants' house and appeared from behind a tree. "What happened?"

"Come," I said without stopping. "I'll tell you on the way."

"On the way where?"

"To the cottage."

DRAKE

THE PULL INSIDE ME GREW STRONGER WITH EACH STEP I TOOK.

Lately, I had been feeling the pull, the tug that I thought was for Thea, more often, stronger, as if it was letting me know something was wrong. As much as I wanted to spend every moment with her, I tried ignoring this feeling. I couldn't simply slip out of the castle whenever I wanted. I was sure that besides Luana, who still played the spy, Alex had put more guards and other vampires to keep an eye on me.

But I couldn't ignore it anymore. I didn't want to.

I missed Thea. I needed to see her.

I sensed her presence and smelled her sweet scent before the cottage appeared in the distance. But she wasn't alone.

I swallowed a growl the moment I saw her servant pacing the porch beside her. It wasn't her fault that he was pushed on to her, but I hated the fact that they were bonded.

"What if he doesn't come?" her servant asked her.

"I wasn't able to send him any notes," she said, her voice soft, worried. "I don't think he'll come."

"Then what are we doing here?"

"Getting away from the mess inside the castle."

"What if Princess Morda comes after you and doesn't find you there?"

"Can you stop with the three hundred questions? It's making me nuts. And that pacing is making me dizzy."

A corner of my lips curled up. At least she didn't take crap from him. Good girl.

Keeran halted a few steps from her. "We should go back before the witches notice you're gone and report it to Princess Morda."

A knot appeared between Thea's brows and she opened her mouth, ready to probably tell him to go to hell, but then she saw me approaching the cottage. "Drake," she whispered, her eyes going wide. "How ... how did you know I was here?"

"I felt it," I said. I glanced at her servant.

He lowered his gaze. "I'll go for a walk," he muttered before stepping down the porch steps and disappearing into the woods.

Thea flung herself at me, wrapping her arms around my neck. "I missed you."

I wound my arms around her waist and kept her pressed to me. "I missed you, too."

Keeping her close to me, I lifted her off the ground and carried her inside the cottage. I closed my eyes, focusing on her scent, on the increased thump of her heart, on the strength of her hold on me. Home. That was how it felt to be with her like this. It didn't matter where we were, where we lived. When she held me like this, I was home.

"I love you," I whispered in her ear.

She pulled back enough to look into my eyes. "What happened?"

"Why? Can't I say that I love you anymore?"

A small smile appeared in her lips. "Of course you can. You should. But you usually don't say it that freely."

It wasn't as if we had had many moments together to know for sure, but she was right.

I sat down on the couch with her on my lap. Still holding her tight, I told her. "Thomas's ghost came to me last night."

"What? Thomas is a ghost?"

I told her he had been trying to contact me since he died, and that he was spying on Alex for me, but I didn't tell her why he hadn't left this world yet. I couldn't.

"I have something to tell you too," Thea said, her voice thin. I listened in silence as she told me about the Blackmarsh coven attack earlier, and about how she felt she needed to protect the coven's heart. "I touched it and it was like it exploded." Her wide eyes seemed as surprised as her voice. I was surprised too, especially as she went on and told me about pairing with Princess Morda to fight the Queen of the Blackmarsh coven. "Queen Sarah ran."

"And her witches?"

"Followed her."

I frowned. "The only explanation I see for all this is that you are meant to be the Queen of the Silverblood coven."

She shook her head. "No, it can't be. I can't be. If for some twisted joke of the universe I am the Queen, then it means I'll have to face Morda, and she'll come after me with everything she has. She will fight me to prove she's stronger. I really don't want that." She swallowed hard. "And I also don't want the responsibility of leading an entire coven."

"I don't like the idea of leading my own coven, but that's what I'll do once we defeat Alex," I told her. "It's what has to be done."

She cupped my face. "But you'll be a great leader."

"Who says you wouldn't be?"

She rolled her eyes. "I'm not the Queen. The Witch Queen is detected once she's born. I wasn't. I am not. Can we change subjects now?"

So darn sexy when she was annoyed.

"If you insist. I met with Luana's pack."

Her entire body tensed. "And?"

"They agreed to help us."

"Just like that?"

"Just like that," I lied. She didn't need to worry about the details. "They will be ready to attack. I need to let them know when."

"How many are they?"

"I don't know the exact numbers, but there were fifty at the meeting to secure the alpha, so I'm guessing a lot."

"Without knowing the exact numbers, we might be going into a lost battle." She chewed her bottom lip. "We might need more allies."

"What about Morda?"

She humphed. "Now that the Blackmarsh coven attacked, she's talking about retaliating. She even mentioned attacking other witch covens. I'm not sure she'll be open to attack a vampire coven."

"You have to try, though, and let me know soon. You know werewolves are volatile and get angry easily. They will soon tire of waiting and back out of our deal."

"I know, I know." She rolled her shoulders. "Can we stop talking about deals and attacks and war for a minute?"

I smiled. "And what do you want to talk about?"

Thea arched an eyebrow. "How about if we don't talk?"

Oh, I liked that.

Surprising me, she hopped from my lap and knelt before me. "Thea?" I reach for her.

She pointed her index finger at me and magic surrounded me. My arms were pushed open and away, like they were kept to the sides by invisible cuffs. "Just ... enjoy."

Slowly, she undid the buttons and zipper from my pants, and I took a sharp inhale. She pulled my pants down and leaned over me. I growled as she closed her mouth around me and sucked hard.

"Hell," I whispered, fighting against the magic holding me in place. I wanted to touch her. I wanted to entwine my fingers in her hair. I wanted to guide her, but oh hell, she didn't need any guidance. She knew exactly what she was doing.

She was driving me crazy.

Crazy for her.

She grazed her teeth over me, she licked, she sucked. Thea clasped her hands on my hips and dipped into me hard, taking me deep. Hell, heat surged in my chest and rushed down my limbs.

I hadn't had much experience as a human, but I remembered how different sex had been once I had become a vampire. As a vampire, sex was more, much more. Vampires felt more, could endure more, could last longer.

And yet, for some reason, it was even better with Thea. Because of the way she made me feel, because of all the heat and ecstasy she brought out of me, I couldn't hold for as long as I wanted it.

I jerked against her magical chains again, wanting to reach for her and carry her to the bed where I could finally be inside her.

I gasped when she bit down on me, then pulled back. "Stop fighting the magic," she whispered.

Slowly, Thea stood, and with her eyes locked on mine, she slipped off her clothes. Hell, she was perfect. With her plump breasts, thin waist, round hips, long legs, her fair, smooth skin, and her golden hair falling around her shoulders like a blanket, she was perfect.

What did I do to deserve a woman like her?

Still holding me with her magic, Thea straddle me.

"Oh, hell," I groaned when she adjusted herself, pressing her pelvis against mine. All the while, she stared into my eyes, making me crazy with the lust I saw in those beautiful gray pools.

She leaned into me and brushed her lips on mine. So soft, so warm. Beyond myself, my eyes fluttered closed and I moaned. Finally, the magic was gone from my arms, and I clasped her nape, holding her close. I crashed my mouth against hers, claiming her every breath. I moved my lips in a sensual, almost frantic rhythm, and I provoked her by brushing my tongue on hers. She moaned.

I snaked a hand to the small of her back and pressed her to me, gluing her breasts on my chest. Here. Right here. That was where she belonged.

Thea rolled her hips, increasing the friction between us. I broke the kiss and drew in a sharp breath.

Taking advantage of that pause, Thea started unbuttoning my shirt. I helped her with it, and then eager to touch her again, I wrapped my arms around her and pulled her to me again. Thea pulled back, and with a smile, she did it again. Her magic wrapped around my wrists and held my arms back.

I growled, but she only smiled wider.

Freaking stunning.

She skimmed her fingers over my chest and abdomen, contouring every muscle on the way. I shivered when her touch went low.

I leaned into her and kissed her neck. I grazed my tongue on her skin, making her shiver.

"Bite me," she whispered.

I stilled. Slowly, I pulled back to look at her. "Are you sure?"

Thea nodded. "I'm sure." She grasped my shoulders, lifted herself a little. With a naughty grin, she lowered herself over me, taking me inside her. I groaned with the sudden pressure and heat rushing through me. She leaned into me, bringing her neck closer to my mouth. "Bite me."

"My pleasure." My fangs flashed, and I bit into her neck.

Thea moaned and moved over me. Up and down, up and down, taking me deeper with each stroke, while her sweet, sweet blood flowed into my mouth, filling me, rushing through me, like pure energy. It was as if I had been plugged to an outlet, and I suddenly had the power to do keep going, to do anything.

That was what she was to me. She was my energy, my life saver, my batteries. Without her, I would stop. Without her, I didn't function. Without her, I was dead. Just a dead vampire.

But with her ... with her, I could be more. With her, I could strive to be more, to be better, to pretend my heart still beat inside me. I could fight, or at least try to.

Moaning, Thea threw her head back. The magic around my wrists faded, and I wrapped my arms around her, wishing I could touch her every second of every day. Forever.

Knowing I had already taken too much, I retracted my fangs and licked Thea's neck to speed up the healing. But she didn't stop moving, she still rode me, up and down, up and down ... it was a sweet torture I was happy to suffer through.

So freaking delicious.

But I wanted more, much more.

I held her tight and stood from the couch.

"Hey!" she protested, holding tight to my shoulders.

I carried her to the bed, where I lowered us, without disentangling our bodies. I pulled back enough to look at her, to see her hair fanned out around her, her beautiful face, her brilliant gray eyes, and the wide smile that was just for me.

She wriggled under me. "Move or I will."

I chuckled. "Your wish is my command."

I thrust into her, burying myself in her. I moved in a slow, but deep rhythm, and Thea moaned, throwing her head back and wrapping her legs around my waist. I loved to feel her like this—under me, arching her back for me, moaning and squirming for me.

I took her mouth with mine, wishing she could melt into me. Together forever. I moved slowly at first, but she was too good. The way her fingers dug in my shoulders, urging me closer, was all it took to make me lose it. I thrust into her faster, deeper, harder. It didn't take long for my ecstasy to build up, but I tried to hold it, enjoying this too much to stop now.

But then Thea slid her hands to my hips, pulling me closer, as if that were possible. "Please," she whispered, a second before breaking into little tremors as her climax exploded.

It was all it took for me to lose it. I thrust one last time and stilled inside her. The wave of ecstasy washed through me, and my body started trembling.

Thea wrapped her arms around my neck and pulled me

to her. I buried my face on the crook of her neck, inhaling her sweet, addicting scent.

"I love you," she whispered in my ear.

If my dead heart could beat ... I dug my elbow on the mattress and propped my head on my hand, so I could look into her eyes. "I love you more."

17

THEA

DRAKE PRESSED HIS LIPS TO MY FOREHEAD. "I'LL SEE YOU soon."

I balled my fist into his shirt, holding him close. "Please, be careful."

"You too." He rested his forehead on mine. "I love you."

"I love you, too," I whispered.

He brushed his lips on mine, dragging a sigh from deep into my chest. I melted into him for a moment, a moment that ended too fast as he pulled back and zipped away with his vampire speed.

I stepped off the porch and glanced around. "Keeran?"

He walked out from behind a tree on the other side of the cottage. "I'm here."

"What were you doing?"

"Just walking around the perimeter of the woods around the cottage, making sure no one had followed us."

"Thank you. For that and for coming with me."

He shrugged. "Not that I have a lot of choice with the bond."

I shook my head. "We'll find a way of breaking it, I promise."

Keeran didn't look convinced. In silence, we both turned away from the cottage and walked back to the coven.

The chaos continued around the mansion. There was no active battle going on, but there was still blood and a few bodies lingering. Witches were carting them away, probably to be burned behind the mansion, and cleaning the floors.

A witch, who had been using her magic to push a body out, saw us approaching. She frowned and spat, "Where have you been?"

Another witch heard it and turned to us too. "Did you run off?"

"I bet she did," another one said. "You were scared and ran off."

A fourth one cackled. "Oh, I would love to see Princess Morda perform the bloodbone ritual on you."

What had I ever done to these witches? It wasn't as if I had been mean before. And I had saved them, twice now—by bringing the heart back and by fighting the queen of the Blackmarsh coven with Morda.

Before I could figure out a good comeback, two witch-guards appeared in front of me. "Princess Morda would like to see you."

My stomach dropped.

The other witches whistled and laughed.

"She'll skin you alive," one of them said.

I wouldn't give them the satisfaction of seeing me tremble. Instead, I lifted my chin high and took deliberate, firm steps as I followed the witchguards to the main hall.

The witchguards halted by the open door, but gestured

for me to continue. When Keeran stepped after me, the witchguards placed their weapons in his way.

"Just Thea," one of them said.

By all that was sacred, this couldn't be good.

I glanced over my shoulder and offered Keeran a small but reassuring smile. "It's okay. Go to my bedroom and wait for me there."

His eyes sparkled with worry, but he bowed his head. "Yes, my lady."

I turned around before he left and stepped into the main hall. The moment I did, the witchguards closed the doors behind me.

"There you are," Morda said, gesturing for me to come closer.

My insides turned over as I faced Morda and the several witches standing around her. Soraya, Adya, Polina, Vera, and a few others.

I stopped a few feet from her and curtsied. "Did you call me, my Princess?"

"I sent for you hours ago. Where were you?"

"I ..." My cheeks warmed and I hoped they believed the lie that was about to spout. "I went out with my servant, Keeran, to hm ... celebrate our victory."

Morda's smile was wide and fatal. "I like that. You helped win the battle and you're working on your duty to this coven. If only all my witches were like you."

She had no idea.

I ignored the hatred shooting from the stares of many of the witches inside the main hall. I wanted to shrug into myself and step behind them, but I kept my ground and posture. "How can I help, my Princess?"

Morda nodded. "I had called a war meeting and wanted you to participate. After all, you saved us twice now."

That was a surprise. I bowed to her. "That would be my honor, my Princess."

All business, Morda turned to Soraya, allowing me to step back and into line with the other witches, and continued, "As I was saying, I think now is the time to attack the Blackmarsh and the Bluemoon covens and prove to them that we cannot be easily crushed."

"They might be waiting for retaliation, my Princess," Polina said.

"They might, but if we don't act now, they will think we're weak and come for us again," Morda said. Her gaze settled on me, and I felt myself freezing all over. "Don't you think, Thea?"

It was now or never.

"With all due respect, my Princess, I might have another idea," I said, praying they didn't see how my hands were shaking. "I think we should attack the vampires instead."

The witches fell on me.

"What?"

"That doesn't make any sense."

"The vampires? We're talking about the witches."

Morda raised her hand, silencing the others. "Thea, explain."

I willed my entire self to remain calm, composed, strong. "Ever since Lord Reynard was murdered, DuMoir Castle hasn't been the same. The vampires are fighting among themselves, and a prince was killed after an argument," I said, stretching the truth. I would spin whatever lie I needed to make sure they realized how crucial my idea was. "They are unstable and disorganized. Prince Alex is now Lord Alex, but before leaving the castle, I found out there was a group strongly against him. They promised an uprising if he came to power." I paused for effect. "If we attacked DuMoir Castle now, the vampires wouldn't stand a chance. And if we took the DuMoir vampires down, it wouldn't be just the other witch covens who feared us. It would be all supernaturals. The Silverblood coven would rule all others."

Morda's eyes sparkled as she processed my words. "That's …"

"Absurd!" Adya snapped.

"Impossible!" Polina said.

"Crazy!" Vera spat.

"Hopeless!" Soraya offered.

"Brilliant," Morda whispered, shocking them all. Me too. "If we overthrow Lord Alex and take the castle for us, no one would dare attack us again." She beamed at me, her smile an odd mix of wicked and exciting. "It's brilliant."

I gulped, hiding my surprise. I had expected more resistance from her. I thought I would have to lie more, to beg, to grovel. Actually, I thought I would have to convince Soraya first, making her believe it would be an easy win from the tactical side.

"My princess?" Soraya asked, sounding almost afraid of Morda. "Think about this for a moment. Our war isn't with the vampires. It's with the witches."

Morda turned to Soraya, her smile changing into a snarl. "Our war isn't with the vampires? Of course it is. It always has been. Despite stealing the coven's heart back, we never got revenge for all we have suffered, for all they put us through for having taken our most powerful item." She let out a long breath. "They must pay!"

Soraya shot me a glare. "You're right, my Princess."

"Get everyone ready," Morda ordered. "We'll attack DuMoir Castle on the second sunrise!"

Soraya bowed. "Yes, my Princess." She scurried out of the main hall, followed by most of the witches.

Morda smiled at me. "You're surprising me, Thea. I didn't know the potential you harbored. Keep up like this and you might become a permanent member of my inner circle."

I lowered my head. "You honor me, my Princess."

She waved me off. "Now go and get some rest. I'll need you strong and ready for the attack."

"Yes, my Princess," I said, bowing once more.

I did my best to maintain my posture and composure while I walked out of the main hall. Keeran was waiting for me in the hallway, even though I had asked him to wait for me in my bedroom. I saw the flash of curiosity and worry once he saw me coming his way. But I gave him the slightest head shake. He understood and fell into step with me.

In tense silence, we made our way to my bedroom. Once we were safe inside, I grabbed a pen and notepad and sank down on the love seat.

"What happened?" Keeran asked, his tone clearly concerned. "What did she want?"

"She wanted to take advantage of our victory and attack the other witch covens," I said, quickly writing a message down. "But I was able to convince her to attack DuMoir Castle instead."

Keeran went rigid. "You did?"

"I did." I was feeling proud of myself, but on edge. The show would work. The war would start. There was no going back now. I folded the note and handed it to Keeran. "Here. Take this to Drake as soon as you can."

He took the note and placed it inside his pocket. "What if I can't reach him again?"

I shook my head. "That's not an option. He has to get that note. Otherwise, he won't be ready. He won't call the werewolves." I took Keeran's hand and squeezed it hard. "Please, find a way to make sure this note gets into Drake's hand."

Keeran pressed his lips together. "I'll do my best."

18

DRAKE

AFTER DRINKING FROM THEA, THE BLOOD FROM THE BOTTLES was almost tasteless. I stared at the full glass in front of me. Plain, that was one word to call it. But still, I had to push it down my throat. I needed my strength if I wanted to be ready to attack.

In the living room, Luana grunted. She had been pacing in front of the couch for the last hour, grunting every few seconds. Her fast heartbeat and breathing told me she was nervous. Anxious. I was too, but I could do nothing about it other than wait for the right moment.

I sighed and my thoughts returned to Thea. She hadn't been this annoying. I mean, yes, she had pissed me off in the beginning, but she had calmed down. Thea used to lie down on the couch, read, and talk to me. She had been my safe haven, and she still had no idea.

Luana wouldn't stop. She paced, she complained, she grunted, she marched up and down the hallway, and she complained some more. I had to refrain from squeezing her neck at least three times a day.

Luana grunted. "This is maddening. You saw her last night. She must have told you when the witches will be ready."

"Thea doesn't know." I had probably told her that several times since I came back from the cottage last night. "She'll send a message when it's time."

She crossed her arms. "So we're supposed to sit here and wait?"

I nodded. "Pretty much."

Luana grunted once more then stormed off. Acting like a teenager, she slammed the door to her bedroom and hid inside.

I sighed. She was nineteen years old, for hell's sake. She was still a teenager. And not much younger than Thea, who had gone through worse.

I had to give these young women credit. Here I was, dealing with upcoming wars when I was almost five hundred years old, and they were only twenty and nineteen.

I felt like an old man. Now all I needed was white hair, a beard, and a beer belly.

A smile spread over my face. Until I remembered I would never grow old.

I didn't like to think about that because it reminded me of Thea. Witches lived long lives. I had heard of some who had been a little over a thousand years old before they passed, but even if Thea lived that long, she would one day die, and I wouldn't.

Not liking the direction of my thoughts, I downed the blood in the glass and went for a walk. Being outside, taking in fresh air, and watching the moon would do me some good and ease my worries, if only for a few minutes.

I was in the second hallway near the main stairs when I sensed him.

Every nerve in my body tensed, and I clenched my teeth.

"Alex," I snarled, once I was sure he was in hearing distance.

In the blink of an eye, he was standing in front of me. "It's *Lord* Alex now." His lips curled into a smug smile. But worse than his grin was the necklace hanging from his neck. I hated seeing Lord Reynard's silver cross pendant, the symbol of our coven, resting against Alex's chest.

I bent at my waist, going low, even lower than I had ever gone for Lord Reynard. "Yes, my Lord," I spat out.

Alex pushed me against the wall, his arm in front of my neck. "Show me respect, worm. I'm your Lord now and you're …" He stared at me from my head to my toes and back. "You're nothing."

I wouldn't fall for his tricks. I wouldn't let him get to me. The moment I retaliated, he would know I had been lying about my lost memories and Thea's control.

He would win.

"If you say so."

"That's right," he said in a low growl. "You're nothing, and you'll always be nothing." I bit my tongue to refrain from saying anything. This was harder than I thought. "Now that I'm Lord, I can do anything I want. I can kill as many humans as I want. Did you know we're having another feast soon?" My eyes widened, but I smoothed my expression before he noticed. He continued, "Of course you don't. You're not a prince anymore. You don't participate in the meetings anymore. You don't have a say in any of it." He smiled. "I was going to have a feast every month, but I think every week serves better. This way, we don't need to drink from bottles. Only fresh. So much better."

Rage grew inside me. What the hell was he thinking? Lord Reynard had asked me to put down a werewolf alpha who didn't mind the humans finding out about supernaturals. Alex was going in the same direction by hosting feasts every week. The humans would notice. It would be hard to erase or change everyone's mind. It was grotesque and wrong.

"If you say so," I said through gritted teeth. What I really wanted was to push him back and break his neck.

He shoved me against the wall. "What's wrong with you? Do something. Show me some emotion. Where's your rage? It seems you're truly nothing." He eased his grip on me. "Oh well. When I take a dozen blood slaves and drain them dry, you won't have a say in it. And when I come for your blood slave, you won't be able to say anything either."

My mind filled with images that made me sick: Thea in his arms in this same corridor as he was about to bite her neck; Thomas crying and jerking at the guillotine and Alex laughing in pleasure.

What would he do to Luana?

I didn't want to know.

The rage erupted, and I pushed him back until he was against the wall and my hands around his neck.

"Don't you dare—"

Alex laughed. "What? Do you think you can stop me?"

He retaliated by spinning us around and shoving me into the wall. Then, he did something I wasn't prepared for.

He bit me.

Alex bared his fangs and sank his teeth in my neck. Pain erupted under my skin.

I had a choice here. To fight back and only hell knew

what would happen. If I fought back, he would make things harder for me. He would probably put more guards by my door, and he would grill Luana. He would punish my men, the same ones he kept away from me.

But if I let him bite me, he would think I admitted he was stronger, he was better. He was the lord of the castle. Biting another vampire was a great show of disrespect, and it was showing Alex I was his bitch. As much as I hated it, I needed Alex off my back for the takeover plan to work.

So I let him bite me.

He pulled back a few second later, licking his lips. "Stay down, dog." With a winning grin, Alex stormed off.

I leaned against the wall, ashamed, but proud of my self-control. I ran a hand over my neck, but it had already stopped bleeding and the holes were closing. Thankfully, I wouldn't have a mark left behind.

Conflicted, I thought about going back to my quarters and lying down on my bed and dreaming about Thea, but that was the coward in me talking, and I wasn't a freaking coward.

Ignoring my hurt pride, I resumed my walk to the gardens.

More guards than usual patrolled the outside of the castle, but they didn't bother me as I made my way to the stone bench where I first kissed Thea. I didn't know why, but I always ended up there.

I sat down on the bench and closed my eyes, conjuring memories of Thea and holding on to them. Better than thinking about what I had let Alex do.

I felt like my honor was slipping between my fingers like water.

"My Prince," Thomas called me.

I snapped my eyes open and stared at the whitish shape forming in front of me. It was odd how I hadn't sensed him coming, but I guess I couldn't sense ghosts.

"Thomas, it's good to see you," I said, being honest. After my encounter with Alex, seeing a friendly face was a nice relief. Even if that friendly face was a ghost. His form looked brighter today. "It seems you're getting the hang of the ghost thing."

He looked down at himself. "It's getting easier, I guess."

I nodded, unsure what to say. He was a ghost, after all, because of me. "So, anything to tell me?"

"Actually, yes, my Prince," he said. "I think I found something."

I held my breath. "What?"

"A rebel camp of vampires."

19

"Do you need anything, Thea?" Morda asked.

Heat warmed my cheeks as all eyes turned to me.

Morda had invited me to breakfast, and this time I was seating on her left side. If the other witches had glared at me the first time, now they were skinning me alive with their heated stares.

I hated being here. And I hated that I was alone. Keeran was still gone. He had left to take the note to Drake and hadn't returned, which made me incredibly sick. What had happened to him? Morda had asked about him once I came into the dining room alone. I lied that I left him resting after an active night. She had seemed pleased.

Ebby wasn't here either. I hadn't seen her since the beginning of the Blackmarsh attack, though I had heard she had helped clean up the mansion and heal the wounded witches.

I set down my coffee mug. "No, my Princess, thank you."

She shook her head once. "There must be something our now twice savior wants."

This had to be a game. She had never offered something, insisted on giving something, to someone. To anyone.

I offered her a confident smile. "I already have all I need, my princess. Thank you."

Seated across the table from me, Soraya scoffed.

Morda ignored her and went on. "Well, my offer stands. If you think of something, let me know. I'll be glad to reward you again."

The rest of breakfast was awkward and tense. I felt like every witch in there would have jumped at the opportunity to beat me up, except for Morda. She looked at me as if I were her best witch and she was proud of me.

Once breakfast was done, Morda stood from her chair and looked at all of us. "Go get ready or rest if you need to, because we leave for the DuMoir Castle in less than twenty hours."

She spun around and sashayed out of the dining room, followed closely by Soraya and two other witchguards. After a few more glares my way, the other witches rose to their feet and walked out of Morda's chambers, talking and whispering about the upcoming attack.

When no one else was looking, I hurried to my bedroom, hoping to find Keeran. But he wasn't there. I hadn't seen him in hours, and the desperation inside me would soon explode and carry me down with it.

I had no idea what had happened. Had Keeran bumped into a werewolf while trying to get past the woods around DuMoir Castle? Had a vampire found him? Had he been able to deliver the message to Drake, but got lost on the way back? Or hurt?

Or worse ...

I didn't think he was dead, because I didn't feel different. I couldn't sense him with our bond, but I could feel its magic and it still held true.

Even so, something wasn't right. I knew something wasn't right.

If Keeran hadn't reached Drake, then Drake didn't know about the attack tomorrow. He wouldn't tell the werewolves. He wouldn't be ready for it. The witches would charge into the castle and win—and Drake would be slaughtered with the rest of the vampires. Morda wouldn't spare him, even if I begged for his life.

We couldn't attack DuMoir Castle tomorrow.

There was only one thing I could think of that would postpone tomorrow's battle.

After constructing a detailed plan, I went to Ebby's bedroom on the other side of the mansion. I wasn't sure if she would be there, but it was my first guess.

I knocked on her door once, twice ... I was turning around to go look for her somewhere else, when the door opened.

"Thea?" Ebby rubbed the sleep out of her eyes. "What are you doing here?"

I gaped at her. Her hair was messy and she was still wearing a nightgown. "Were you sleeping?" She nodded. "But it's almost noon."

"I heard Princess Morda ordered everyone to rest, so that's what I was doing."

"Sorry." I pushed her in and closed the door behind me. "But we have no time for that."

"What's going on?" She blinked. The sleepiness faded away. "What happened?"

I bit my lower lip. "I need your help."

"What for?"

"You need to distract the witchguards for me."

Ebby crossed her arms and tilted her head. "And what stupid thing are you going to do?"

"I'm going to steal the heart of the coven."

20

I followed Thomas to the village outside the castle, while trying to wrap my head around everything he had told me.

Apparently, a group of vampires lived in one of the houses in the village. Some still lived in the castle, but met with the others often to discuss plans and express their rage. They started the rebel group years ago, when some of them disagreed with Lord Reynard's rules. Now under Alex's thumb, they were infuriated. Talks about revolts and takeovers were constant among them, but because their numbers weren't large, they kept it all quiet. They were more like a support group.

"You can change that," Thomas said when telling me about them. "You have a plan; you have other allies. If they join you, they will have a purpose; they will have a strategy."

That sounded too good to be true.

Thomas guided me to one of the last houses in the village, where there was an antique store in the front. The house was similar to the rest of the village. Wood painted a shade of brown, two stories, dark brown roof, and a big glass window in the front displaying the store inside. But unlike the other houses, this one had all its lights out.

Thomas stopped by the back door and glanced at me. "I have to tell you something before we go in."

I tensed. "What?"

"These vampires ... they are weak and a little crazy."

"What?" I repeated, certain I hadn't heard him right.

But Thomas didn't answer me. He disappeared through the solid wall. A moment later, the door opened and a blond vampire stared at me.

"Look who we have here," the vampire said, smiling. His fangs were out. "An ex-prince."

It took me a moment to process his appearance. His long hair looked like a bird's nest, his skin was still smooth and young, but his face had a rough edge to it, as if he had aged a little since becoming a vampire. When he took a few steps back to allow me to enter, I noticed his gait—he walked as if he were limping, which was impossible.

Then I took in all the vampires in the small and almost furniture-less living room. All of them looked as disheveled and savage as the blond vampire—though still beautiful and lethal.

The shine in their wide eyes screamed lunatic.

I wasn't so sure it had been a good idea coming here.

"I'm Prince Drake," I said, loud and clear. The title didn't have any weight nowadays, but I would use it if it helped gain some fans and favors.

The blond vampire pointed to himself. "Lark, and this is Remi." He gestured to a large, black vampire standing on the other side of the room. "We're the leaders here."

"Your ghost lackey told us you wanted to meet us," Remi

said. Once upon a time, it seemed he had an accent, but it had been mostly lost over the years. "What for?"

What the hell was I doing here? Could I trust these crazy vampires? I already had the werewolves and hopefully the witches on my side. I didn't need two dozen crazy vampires.

"Never mind," I muttered, turning to the door.

Lark stepped in my way and slapped a big hand on the door. "I don't think so."

I frowned. "Excuse me?"

Remi appeared right behind me. "You've seen too much. We can't let you leave."

They were crazy. "Seen too much? What have I seen?"

"You know about us," Remi said, smiling wide so I could see his exposed fangs. "You know where to find us. That's too much."

I stilled. "And what are you going to do about it?"

"We're going to kill you," Lark snarled.

Both leaders made a go for me. Besides being better fed and healthier, I was older than them, which made me stronger.

I stepped to the side, dodging their attacks. I punched Lark's chin and kicked Remi's chest. They kept coming at me, teeth bared and hands shaped like claws. Just like animals.

But their lack of real fight training was to my advantage.

Lark tried to punch my face. I ducked and punched his ribs instead—five quick jabs that pushed him back. Then Remi tried to land some kicks on my side. I spun at an angle and landed a powerful side kick to his hips that sent him sliding backward.

They didn't give up. Lark and Remi came at me again. Though I was focused on them, I noticed the crowd closing in on the fight. Were they afraid I would escape? Would they try to stop me?

Try was a big word tonight.

Because they kept trying to hit me—to no avail.

Tired of these games, I bared my teeth and punched Lark in the middle of his chest, putting a lot of my strength into it. The vampire flew across the room. He slammed into the built-in shelves along the wall, breaking them.

Remi's punch grazed my jaw. With a groan, I pushed his arm away, then stepped into him and gave him a knife hand strike to the neck. He coughed as I spun around and landed an elbow strike to his chest. He stumbled back, but I held his wrist. I swept my foot around his ankle and he went down. Still holding his arm, and twisting it, I stepped onto his neck.

Then the other vampires were on me.

Seeing their leaders out, they charged at me. They weren't strong, but the determination in their eyes, in their coiled muscles, and the roughness of their movements, spoke to me. Even though there was no chance they would defeat me, they didn't stop trying.

Distracted by the other vampires, I only noticed Lark and Remi coming at me just as their hands closed around my arms and wrists. They pulled me in opposite directions, forcing me to stand straight.

The other vampires took a step back and watched as their leaders gloated about overpowering a prince.

This was pathetic. Did they really think they had me?

I forced my arms down and stepped back. Lark and Remi lost their hold on me. Before they could recover from the surprise, I landed a roundhouse kick to the back of Remi's head, making him stumble forward, and gave Lark an arm lock, then pulled his back against my chest, my hand tight on his neck.

Everyone froze , including Remi.

Right now, they knew that if they moved in the wrong direction, if they breathed too loud, it would end Lark.

They were one unprepared bunch, but I couldn't deny I was impressed with their instinct and determination.

"Hear me out." I dropped my hand from Lark's neck. "I came here looking for allies."

Remi crossed his arms, on the defensive. "Allies?"

"Yes." I sighed. I had to be as lunatic as they were to be considering this, but it seemed better than to fight my way out. Let them burn this energy somewhere else. Like a real battlefield. "I plan on overthrowing Alex soon."

Remi's and Lark's eyes bulged.

"How?" Lark asked.

"I have a few allies waiting. They will come when I call. But I could use more help." I looked around. "You just proved to me you're strong and determined. If you agree to help me, I'll get more blood to you to help you build your strength." Again, probably not a great idea, but if they joined me, I would rather have them ready to do real damage.

"And what do we gain from this?" Remi asked.

"You wouldn't need to hide anymore," I said. "If I become lord, you could come back to a luxurious life inside the castle."

Lark spat at the floor. "We don't want any lord of the castle."

"What do you mean?"

"There's only one way we'll join you," Remi said.

Lark nodded. "Tell us you'll abolish the monarchy and we'll join you."

That was unexpected. "No monarchy?"

"Exactly," Remi said. "No lords, no kings, no princes. We want everyone free. We want no laws or regulations. And we want to hunt for humans in the wild."

In the wild? Humans didn't wander in the wild. Did he mean going into towns and attacking them? That was too much.

The same determination that shone in their eyes when they were fighting me was now stamped on their faces. All of them. The only way to have them join me was to lie to them.

"That ... that sounds like a good idea, actually." Thomas appeared by my side, his eyes wide. I ignored him and went on. "If we overthrow Alex, I'll make sure it's the end of the monarchy. We'll be all free to do whatever we want."

Grinning and showing me their fangs, Lark and Remi extended their hands at me.

"Then we have a deal," Lark said.

I shook their hands. "Thomas will let you know when we're ready to attack."

Thomas shrank under their crazed gazes.

After a few more details and unsaid threats, Lark opened the door and let us leave.

The village was quiet and mostly dark. It only really functioned when we had feasts. Now that Alex held them each week, I had no idea what he planned to do about it.

Everything was falling apart.

Halfway to the castle, Thomas mustered the courage to ask me the question I knew he was dying to.

"You lied to them about dissolving the monarchy, right?"

I nodded once. "Right." Which I wasn't proud of. I had always upheld my morals and honor above everything else. Lying was the exact opposite. "As much as it would be grand to live in a world without a monarchy, every society needs a leader and rules, otherwise it would be chaos." Perhaps we could consider some other kind of government for our society, but that was a worry for the future. If we ever got there.

"Then what are you going to do?"

"Once I assume power, I'll seize them. They will have a choice: Either join us or they will be banished forever."

Thomas looked down. "Just please don't become a dictator. An oppressing leader."

I sighed, afraid of exactly that. "I'll try."

21

THEA

THOUGH WE HAD BEEN ORDERED TO BED EARLY THE PREVIOUS night, I barely slept a wink. I was too anxious to rest and sleep. I still hadn't heard from Keeran, and so far, it seemed Morda hadn't found out the heart was missing.

I was able to convince Ebby to help me. I taught her an illusion spell, and while she performed that and distracted the witchguards guarding the tower, I slipped past them and stole the heart. As usual, it beat faster once I touched it, and with its power in my hands, it was even easier to get out of the tower and the mansion undetected.

I took the heart of the coven to the cottage where Drake and I always met, and after storing it inside a velvet sack, I buried it deep in the ground at the roots of a thick tree behind the property.

Here, no one would find it.

Despite everything plaguing my thoughts, I felt confident as I went down to the main hall. I was expecting to find Morda going crazy, screaming about the heart and that the attack would be postponed until we found it.

I crossed the open doors and stopped in my tracks.

Witches walked around in gowns, and witchguards wore their battle leather uniform. Standing by her tall chair, Morda wore a leather gown like that.

What?

"Thea," Morda said, grinning at me. "There you are."

The hundreds of witches in the main hall glanced at me, but didn't stop buckling potions and weapons to the straps in their clothes.

By all that was sacred …

Swallowing my surprise, I rushed to Morda's side. "Morning, my Princess." I curtsied in a haste. She couldn't know I had expected the battle to be canceled by now. "Sorry for having slept in."

She waved me off. "We have a little time before we go. You should get ready, though."

"Yes, my Princess." My mind reeling, I turned to leave.

"Thea, wait," Morda called. I froze. Slowly, I glanced over my shoulder. Morda gestured for me to come closer. My heart pumped against my ribs as I went to her. "Something happened last night," she whispered.

I could feel the blood draining from my face. "W-what is it?"

"The coven's heart was stolen again," she said, still whispering. I gasped, pretending surprise. "I have a group of witches out looking for it."

So she already knew about it. "But … what about the battle? Can we attack if we don't have the power of the heart with us?"

Morda opened her arms wide. "Can't you feel it?"

I frowned. "What?"

"Our power. The heart's power. Even with the heart gone, our power is still in full flux."

How was that possible? Unless ... unless Drake was right, and I was the witch queen. The coven would be able to channel the heart's power through me.

I inhaled deeply. "I-I don't understand."

She grabbed my wrist and her eyes sparkled. "It must be because one of us has finally conceived a child. The witch queen. Shame we don't have time to perform pregnancy checks right now. I would love to know who's carrying such a child. Anyway, the child must be channeling the power of the heart back to the rest of the coven, even if the heart isn't here."

If only Morda knew that it wasn't a baby, but me.

"That's fantastic," I said, forcing a smile.

"I think so, too."

I lowered my head. "If you let me, my Princess, I'll go get ready now." What I really needed was to go back to my bedroom and think. There was too much going on—and not in the right direction.

"Wait," Morda said. I frowned at her. "I have a surprise for you."

What now?

Morda snapped her fingers. From the side door, two witchguards dragged a badly wounded and beaten man.

My heart stopped. "Keeran ..."

"Your servant was found trying to escape the estate, despite the bond I cast over you two," she said, her tone chilling.

I stared at her. She thought I wasn't involved in this? "W-what?"

Soraya appeared from behind me, and showed me her

predatory smile. "He was found in the woods outside the estate. Apparently, he was attacked by wolves prior to being found."

No, no, no.

The werewolves had Drake's note. The werewolves had been expecting me to make contact; maybe they thought this was it. The witches and the werewolves would march into DuMoir Castle with Drake being unprepared for it.

"Bring him forward," Morda ordered.

The witchguards dragged Keeran to the center of the room. As if it had been rehearsed, the hundreds of witches closed around him in a wide circle, with Morda, Soraya, a handful of witchguards, and Keeran and me in the middle.

My hands shook, my breathing grew erratic. By all that was sacred ...

"This will be fun." Soraya winked at me before getting closer to Keeran.

The witchguards pushed Keeran to his knees. He fell forward, too weak to keep himself up, but the hold of the witches in his arms and shoulders kept him up.

Morda halted in front of him. "Keeran, for your attempt at escape and betrayal, I sentence you to death."

I swallowed a gasp.

No, no, no.

Morda lifted her hand, palm turned to him, and light shone from her hand. My feet moved without my consent, but before I could do anything, Keeran let out a roar. Magic burst from him like a jet of red flames.

The witchguards holding Keeran fell to the ground, screaming in pain. Too fast, Morda cast a shield around us, but it broke in contact with Keeran's power.

"He's a warlock!" Soraya cried in horror.

"Kill him!" Morda screamed.

All the witches raised their hands toward him.

No, this wasn't supposed to go down like this.

I channeled my power, the heart's power, and it filled me like an avalanche. Without moving an inch so I wouldn't get caught, I cast a protective shield around him.

The witches' magic hit the shield, causing it to tremble, but I could feel it. It wouldn't break. Not when I had the heart's power flowing through me.

Holy shit, I was the witch queen.

Keeran rose to his feet, and using his magic, he threw a few black bolts at the witches, forcing them to retreat and open the circle. I kept the shield up around him even when he ran out of the mansion and the witches went after him.

"Let him go!" Morda's voice echoed off the walls.

The witches stopped. I frowned, but didn't break the shield around Keeran even after he had crossed the gardens and reached the forest. I would keep it up until I didn't sense him anymore ... and who knew when that would be? With the heart's power in me, I felt like anything was possible.

But I did sense something: When Keeran's power manifested, our bond was broken. I couldn't feel anything tying us to each other now. He was free to flee, and I was free to go to Drake.

Soraya faced Morda. "My Princess, we need to kill him," she barked. Soraya wasn't used to losing.

"We don't have time to chase after a rogue warlock right now," Morda spat. Her movements were short and hard. She was furious. "Not when we have a castle to attack."

"We're still going to DuMoir Castle?" Soraya asked.

"Yes." Morda rolled her shoulders and raised her chin high. "Get ready, my witches, we march in fifteen minutes."

Panic building in my chest, I slipped out of the main hall. If anyone stopped me, I would lie that I was going to my bedroom to get ready for battle. Thankfully, the witches were all too busy and no one saw as I ran from the mansion.

22

DRAKE

PACING MY LIVING ROOM SEEMED TO BE A PREFERRED PASTIME. This time, though, it wasn't Luana, but me. Ever since coming back from talking to the rebel vampires last night, I had felt anxious, more anxious than before.

All that was missing now was Thea's signal. Once she contacted me and let me know the witches were coming, I would tell the werewolves and the rebel vampires. I would then try talking to princes Cain, Phelps, and Gray about what was to come. Hopefully, they would listen to me; they would support me as they once had done.

If all went down as it was supposed to, Alex and his allies didn't stand a chance.

Soon, this castle would be mine, and I would restore order and peace.

I shuddered, dreading the weight of it all. It would be a boulder permanently settled on my shoulders, a boulder I had agreed to, and yet, I wasn't sure I was ready for it. I didn't think I would ever be ready for it.

To alert the werewolves, I needed Luana here, and she

had been gone for hours now. I had assumed she had gone to Alex for her daily duty—reporting on me and my activities. According to her, all she told him was that I sulked in my chambers, dragged my feet around the garden while grumbling about my miserable life, drank her blood, and tried to persuade the other princes that Alex was bad news. The last one wasn't a lie, but it hadn't been that simple either.

I wouldn't risk talking to other princes about my plans unless I was sure they would stand by my side, or the attack was imminent. And even then, who knew? Most of the princes had always been fickle and supported whoever gave them more power.

I sighed and stared at the door.

If she wasn't coming, then I would go after her. Who cared? If Alex saw me looking for her, even better. This way he would believe I was really into her—and too distracted to do anything.

In fact, I would go banging on Alex's door.

But, as I was going down the stairs, I heard rapid footsteps and rushed words. Several guards rushed past me.

What was going on?

I turned, sensing Prince Dorian coming this way. "What happened?"

He paused beside me. "We're under attack."

"W-what?"

No, it wasn't time yet. This was wrong.

"Well, we'll be soon," he said. "Werewolves are coming from one side and witches from the other. They will be here in a matter of minutes." He frowned, puzzled. "It seems like an organized attack." Without another word, he ran down the stairs, probably to meet the other princes and organize our defenses.

Hell ... So much for planning and trying to be prepared.

I went back a few steps, and after making sure I was alone, I called upon Thomas.

His shape took form in front of me. "My Prince," he said, sounding out of breath. "I was just coming to warn you—"

"The werewolves and witches are coming."

"Yes." He tilted his head. "Wasn't Thea supposed to let you know about that?"

"She was," I whispered. My chest constricted. "Something must have gone wrong." I could waste time worrying about that, or I could act. "Call the rebels ," I told him. "It's time."

He bowed and said, "Yes, my Prince," before disappearing again.

New sounds filled the castle—the rush of footsteps, the yell of orders, the clanking of armor.

I could join them and pretend to be on their side, or I could slip out of the castle and join the werewolves or the witches. Perhaps I could find Thea and stand with her.

Or I could go looking for Alex and finish this quick.

I took a step down the stairs when I felt him—Alex was coming.

I stood tall atop of the stairs and waited for him.

Not ten seconds later, he was standing at the base of the stairs. Hands curled into fists, he snarled at me. "I don't know how, but I'm sure you're to blame for this surprise attack."

I shrugged. "What if I am?"

Alex bared his fangs. "I will kill you."

"I would like to see you try," I snarled.

I lunged down at him and he jumped up at me. We met halfway in the air. Alex had his hands up to grab me, but I curled my knees into my chest and pushed my legs out, kicking him with both feet in the chest. Alex went careening back down the stone steps.

He groaned but came right back at me. And I went at him.

I punched him hard—and he did the same.

We exchanged blows, and all I could think of was how much I wanted to break his nose, break his chin, break him. Even though I was raised to be a prince, a general of sorts in Lord Reynard's army, I avoided fighting if I could. How would we have a peaceful and harmonious society if we kept fighting, and fighting among ourselves?

I had fought a lot in my long life, but it had been because I had to.

Just like now.

I had to fight Alex. I had to kill him. Otherwise, he would forever drive our society down a rabbit hole, where it would be impossible to rescue it from.

Unfortunately, Alex wasn't like the rebel vampires. He was as old as I was, and well fed and healthy. Our strength and stamina were almost the same.

Baring my fangs, I punched him hard in the jaw. Alex's head snapped to the side with a loud crack. Red rage flashed in his eyes before he pushed me back hard against the stone wall.

"How about we repeat the other night?" Alex snapped his teeth at my face. "How about being my bitch again?"

"In your dreams." I shoved my hand in his chest, and dug it in.

I would have buried my fingers in his body and carved out his heart if he hadn't retreated, eyes wide.

A loud boom resonated through the castle, and a moment later, the walls shook.

"They are here!" someone yelled from downstairs. "Get ready!"

If it had been the werewolves, or the witches, or both, who had arrived, I didn't know. And right now, I didn't care.

All I cared about was finishing the poor excuse for a vampire in front of me.

I took advantage of the distraction and jumped at Alex. He didn't see it coming and was completely taken aback when I landed several good hits to his face. He retreated again, but I went with him, until he was pinned along a tall built-in shelf with lots of decorations.

"Get off me," Alex roared, slamming a picture frame over my head. Then a vase, next a jewelry box, a marble ball, and other things. Until he grabbed the shelf and broke off a piece of wood. First, he broke the wide board on my head, making me dizzy, then he grabbed a smaller piece and pointed at me like a stake.

Panic rose into me as he took advantage of my dizziness and pushed me down, stake in hand.

He knelt on top of my chest and leaned into me. "Goodbye, Prince Drake."

He raised the stake. I readied myself to push him back, to throw him away, to punch him, to fight back, damn it. But before I could react, magic rushed over the stairs like an electric current, and Alex flew across the stairs.

I propped myself on my elbows and saw one of the most beautiful sights of my life: a blond witch with brilliant, long hair, wearing a black gown, coming up the stairs.

Thea was here.

23

THEA

WHEN I SAW ALEX ON TOP OF DRAKE WITH THAT DAMN improvised stake in his hands, my heart stopped. Rage and magic filled my veins, and I blasted the bastard off my love.

"Thea ..." Drake shot up to his feet.

I ran to him. He opened his arms wide, and when I bumped into him, he wrapped his arms tight around me. He rested his face on my neck and inhaled deeply. "I've missed you."

"I missed you too," I whispered.

I pulled back and glanced at him. There were wounds on his face that were already healing, but I wanted to kiss and heal each of those bruises myself.

"Bitch," Alex shouted, coming at us.

I had almost forgotten about him.

Almost.

I raised my hand and the bastard froze in place. Before, this spell would have been impossible on a powerful vampire like him, but since finding out my connection to the coven's heart, I was nearly unstoppable—something that scared the daylights out of me.

"Nice," Drake said, glaring at Alex.

"You bitch!" Alex jerked against my power, but he could do nothing now. He glanced from Drake to me and back to Drake. "I knew there was something going on. I knew she hadn't spelled you. I knew you two were working together."

"What do you want? An award for being smart?" I asked, remembering how much I hated this man.

Beside me, Drake chuckled. "Hell, I love you." He pressed a soft kiss to my temple.

Alex gagged.

I lifted my hand, and my power wrapped around his neck, making him gag.

With a sigh, I let go of Drake. I picked up the stake from the steps and handed it to Drake. "Here. Finish this."

Holding my gaze, Drake took the stake from me and nodded. He turned to his nemesis.

Alex jerked more as he realized what was about to happen. "Drake ... no," he croaked. "Please."

Drake stood in front of a helpless Alex. "Now you beg?" He glanced at me over his shoulder. "Drop him."

I knew what he wanted. He didn't want to cowardly stake Alex. He wanted to give the bastard the chance to fight back. So be it.

I pulled my magic back and Alex fell to the floor, slamming his knees on the stone steps. Drake grabbed Alex's hair and pulled his head back. "Any last words?"

"I'll see you in hell," Alex muttered.

"I'm sure you will, but in several thousand years." Fast like lightning, Drake pierced Alex's chest with the stake.

The vampire let out a gasp. His eyes rolled back and his head lolled forward.

Drake stepped back, letting go of Alex. The body fell on the steps and Drake stayed there, staring at it. I stepped to his back and wound my arms around his waist, resting my cheek on his shoulder.

"It's over now," I whispered.

Drake inhaled deeply. "This part is." He spun inside the circle of my arms. "But there's still the chaos in the rest of the castle for us to deal with."

The sounds of the battle were everywhere. Soon, we would have witches and werewolves and vampires all around us.

Drake unhooked my arms from his waist and slipped his hands in mine. "We should go out there and see what the damage is so far."

I didn't want any more battles or blood, but I knew he was right. We had started this; we needed to end it.

Hand in hand, Drake and I went down the three sets of stairs and found the first level of the castle in complete chaos.

Witches and vampires and werewolves fought each other —no allies.

Drake tugged on my hand. We ran to the right, toward the main ballroom. On the way, we dodged some fights and had to throw some punches to get through. We halted by one of the side doors and surveyed the area.

It was incredible how everyone was focused on attacking; they didn't even see us standing here.

I wondered if my power would allow me to create walls and separate the groups behind them, so we could talk like mature creatures. Even if I could, I was sure they didn't want to talk.

They wanted blood.

Drake pulled me to the left toward a group of werewolves. A few of them hadn't turned yet.

"Ulric," Drake said, approaching a tall guy with leather pants. From his stance and powerful mien, I was sure he was the alpha. "We need to talk."

Ulric smiled at Drake. "Prince Drake! Where have you been?"

"Dealing with Alex."

"Oh, so the Lord of the castle is gone."

"Yes." Drake squeezed my hands. "Listen, I might have a plan to push the witches back."

Ulric tilted his head and narrowed his eyes at us. "I don't care about your plans right now, Prince."

"Then what's your plan?"

Ulric stalked to us, followed by two big men whom I assumed were his betas. I channeled my magic, keeping it at my fingertips in case we needed it.

"I'm done with you, " he said. "My wolves and I are on our own. We'll take the castle for ourselves."

Drake tensed beside me. "That's not what we agreed on!"

Ulric shrugged. "I advise you run before I send my wolves after you, too."

Drake's gaze shift to a young woman standing several feet behind the alpha. "What's going on, Luana?"

So that was his new blood slave. She looked pretty. Jealousy blossomed in my chest, but I pushed it away.

Luana looked down. "I'm sorry, Drake. I'm loyal to my pack."

Drake gritted his teeth and curled his hands into fists. I felt his muscles coiling, his body getting ready to attack.

Careful, I hooked my hand on his arm. "Don't, Drake," I whispered. "We can find another way."

Then, a weird group of vampires invaded the ballroom.

I frowned, watching them. Messy hair, crumpled clothes, rough expressions, wild shine in their eyes.

"Come on," Drake said, tugging my arm.

In the blink of an eye, we were on the other side of the ballroom facing two of those vampires.

"Get out of our way," a black vampire said.

I felt Drake's chest rumbling with an inaudible growl. "Not you too."

"Whatever you're saying, just stop," a blond vampire said. "And get out of our way."

"What about our deal?" Drake asked. He was holding back his temper.

The black vampire smiled wide. "You took out Alex. Congratulations."

"Now, we're satisfied," the blond one said. He opened his arm and gestured to the room. "This is just how we like it. No rulers, no rules ..."

"If you don't want to become vampire food, I suggest you move out of our way," the black vampire said with a snarl.

Sure he was about to fight those vampires, I grabbed Drake's arm and pulled him back. "Let's go."

"Where?" he whispered to me, though he was watching the weird vampires creeping around the room. "If they don't support me, I can't win." He finally looked at me. "I can't win alone."

I placed a hand on his cheek. "You're not alone. You have me. Forever. But I think this battle might be lost. We need to get out of here before it's too late. We'll come up with a new plan. We'll—"

A new boom shook the room.

We all stared at where the explosion came as Morda and her witches marched into the ballroom.

She was staring straight at me, an evil glint in her eyes and a wicked smile on her lips.

She had the coven's heart in her hand.

The floor went out from under my feet, and I felt like I was falling in a black abyss.

No.

How? Where? When?

Ebby appeared at her side, smiling as wickedly as Morda.

I took a step forward, trying hard to fight the truth of the sight in front of me. "What's going on?"

"Oh, dear Thea ..." Morda's voice carried through the room, sending a shock wave through me. Through everyone. The fighting had paused for her. "The moment you came back alive from your suicide mission, I knew something was wrong."

"How could a weak witch such as yourself survive a lair full of vampires?" Ebby said, her shrill tone sending a chill down my spine. This was not the Ebby I had come to know.

Question was: Had I really known her?

"Because of my dear Ebby," Morda continued, "I've known about everything since the beginning. I know about your vermin vampire lover—" She wrinkled her nose at Drake. "—about your escapades to meet him, and about your plan to overthrow the castle and use my coven to help you."

Feeling like a part of my innocent heart had been ripped from me, I glanced at Ebby. "Cheers to you for fooling me so well."

Ebby shrugged. "It was fun. And now because of you, I'll be in Princess Morda's inner circle."

For some reason, I didn't believe that. Morda was using her, promising her beautiful lies she didn't intend to keep. But that wasn't my problem.

"Thea Harrington," Morda said. "For your treachery, I condemn you to death ... by my own hands."

I stood my ground and lifted my chin at her. "You cannot kill me."

Morda scoffed. "And why is that?"

I lifted my hands and channeled my power. The heart's power. In Morda's hand, the heart thrummed and shone. Red light spilled from it like a spiraling snake, coming to me. Morda gasped as the light became blue halfway and gathered at my open palms.

The snake coiled around my wrists and arms and shoulders. It blend into my skin, filling me with power I never imagined I would one day possess.

Morda's face blanched.

I smiled at her. "Because I'm the Witch Queen."

24

DRAKE

THE HORROR AND SURPRISE IN PRINCESS MORDA'S FACE WAS almost comical. However, the knowing grin on Thea's lips sent a chill up my arms. I knew she was playing here, trying to intimidate Morda by pretending to be as insane and evil. Nevertheless, I didn't like to see her like this.

"That's ... that's impossible," Morda muttered. "You can't be the witch queen."

"Why not?" Thea summoned a small blue flame to her hand. She tossed it from palm to palm, playing with it. "Because you're supposed to be?"

Morda opened her mouth. Then, she snapped it shut and curled her hands into tight fists. "I'll prove you're not the witch queen."

A black spark shot out from Morda's hand directly at Thea.

As if a play button had been pressed, the fighting in the ballroom resumed. The vampires, the werewolves, and the witches attacked. It was chaos as everyone fought for themselves. No allies, no sides. Just survival.

I wanted to help Thea with Morda, but I was kept busy by fighting the other witches, who were trying to interfere in the big fight dominating most of the room.

With half of my focus on Thea's fight and half on my own, I was sure to get hurt in no time.

But I couldn't stop watching them.

Thea looked every bit a true queen while she fought Morda, matching the princess strike for strike.

Still holding tight to the coven's heart, Morda shot black sparks at Thea.

Like a boss, Thea waved her hand and the sparks faded into smoke. Gritting her teeth, Morda cast black flames and threw them at Thea. Thea conjured a faint blue shield in front of herself. The flames exploded on the shield and went out—and the shield held strong, even when Morda cast flame after flame and continued sending them Thea's way.

Morda took a step back, struggling with Thea's newfound power.

I smiled.

Tired of being on the defensive , Thea dropped the shield and cast a flame of her own. Morda barely had time to react. She scurried out of the way, and the flame whooshed an inch from her head.

Morda let out a shriek and threw her hands out. A dark wave appeared from the ground, rising high and going for Thea.

Thea joined her palms, then opened her arms wide. The wave parted and continued rolling past Thea, washing over the vampires and werewolves and witches behind her—and burning them.

Morda stared, her mouth hanging open.

Thea acted. She threw blue flames at Morda, who cast a

shield in front of herself, but when the third flame exploded into it, the shield broke.

"That can't be," Morda uttered. Was she finally coming to terms that Thea was the witch queen? Or would she keep denying it?

Morda squeezed the coven's heart. She wasn't the witch queen, but as a Silverblood witch, she could still use the heart's power.

Morda's eyes shone red and a wicked grin appeared on her lips. She held her hand up and red sparks flew out of her palm—thicker than her black ones. It was the heart giving her strength.

Thea waved her hand in front of her, trying to make them fade again, but it took longer this time, and she couldn't make them all disappear. One of the sparks exploded on her shoulder.

I stilled and the witch in front of me landed a nice side-kick on my ribs, robbing me of air. I didn't know what I hated more: when witches fought with magic, which was hard to battle against, or when they came in for a physical fight. Because they shouldn't rely only on magic, most of them knew how to fight—and that was my department.

Swallowing a scream, Thea stumbled back. She created a shield to protect herself, and to take in a breath—she looked as shocked by her injury as I was—but Morda's sparks were too powerful now. On the fourth spark, the shield broke.

Morda threw more sparks, more flames, more bolts. Thea was doing her best to dodge them all while still sending out spells of her own.

Morda gathered her power and threw a big red bolt at Thea. I could see the shine of sweat on Thea's forehead when she closed her hands into fists, then let her hands and arms open, breaking the bolt into two and sending them out.

The two bolts hit the balcony on the second floor of the ballroom, breaking the railing and some of the floor. The metal and concrete fell to the ground, shaking the room once more.

Everyone stopped for a second to assess what was going on, but Morda didn't stop. She took advantage of the distraction and squeezed the heart again, summoning more of its power.

Thea bent over, gasping. Morda was taking the power, and in turn hurting and weakening Thea.

They exchanged more blows, but I could see it clear as crystal. Since she didn't have the heart, Thea couldn't sustain the power for long. Though I believed she still had a lot to give, she couldn't fight forever.

The opposite from the rest of the fighting going on in this castle. The vampires and werewolves and witches were hurt, but with their enhanced stamina, their fight could go on forever.

We had to find a way to end this.

I stared at the broken pieces of metal and concrete on the floor.

Half distracted, I didn't see a werewolf lunging at me. Hell, I didn't have time to waste. I focused all my strength and grabbed the werewolf by its side, taking in handfuls of fur. With a growl, I threw the werewolf across the room.

Then I ran to Thea.

"Finish this," I told her.

She cast a shield in front of us and looked at me. "How?"

This close, she looked even more tired, with clammy skin, dark circles under her eyes, and shaking hands. The wound on her shoulder was charred over, but there was a steady trickle of blood going down her arm.

Hell …

I pointed to the broken balcony. "Destroy the castle and we'll flee."

"But we have to finish this."

I grabbed her hand and squeeze. "Live to fight another day, remember?"

Her gray eyes looked pained, but she nodded.

She turned to her shield and reinforced it.

Then, she took a long breath and raised her hands over her head. She shot blue sparks at the ceiling and the pillars across the room.

The castle shook …

Everyone stilled.

Then, it began to crumble.

A big piece of ceiling fell right between Morda and Thea, sending dust up in the air.

Screams filled the room and chaos returned as some fought and some ran.

I took Thea's hand again and tugged. "Let's go."

Thea stayed put. "Morda has the heart …"

"I know," I said. This couldn't be easy for her. "We'll get it back later. I promise."

When I tugged again, Thea didn't resist.

We weaved through fighting vampires and werewolves, fleeing witches, fallen bodies, and crumbling concrete.

Twice, pillars and walls fell inches from our heads.

We navigated the hallways and ran toward the foyer, where we halted.

The werewolves were there, fighting the rebel vampires.

The main stairs shook and a piercing noise echoed through the air when it broke and fell to the side.

A big black wolf transformed back into a human. "Retreat!" Ulric shouted.

The wolves ran.

All of them except for Luana.

She was in her human form, a lot of dust and blood covering her naked body, and a big piece of concrete on her foot.

"Help me!" she yelled. "Ulric, help me!"

Ulric paused and glanced at her. "Thank you for being a loyal wolf," he said before transforming and running out.

"No!" Her screamed broke with a sob.

Two of the rebel vampires noticed her there, incapable of moving, and advanced on her.

I didn't think.

I lunged at them and ripped their heart out in two seconds flat.

When I turned, Thea was kneeling beside Luana. "You'll be alright." She looked at me. "Help me here." I frowned, but didn't move. "Drake." Thea's voice hardened. "Help me move this stone."

"Why should I?" I spat. "She betrayed me."

"I'm sorry," Luana cried. "I didn't have a choice."

"Drake," Thea started. "We can argue about that later. Now help me because I won't leave her here to die, not like this."

Thea and her good heart …

I sighed and crouched down. The boulder was big and heavy, but I was able to lift it enough for Thea to pull Luana's leg from underneath it. Like I had done before, I took off my shirt and handed it to Thea. She covered Luana's body, then I picked Luana up in my arms.

A white blob appeared by my side, startling me.

"This ceiling is breaking," Thomas said, pointing up.

"Thomas!" Thea cried, her eyes wide.

"Hi, Thea." He smiled at her, but then stared back at me. "You have three seconds to get out of here before being squashed."

With unspoken agreement, Thea and I took off with Thomas floating by our side and Luana half-dead in my arms.

We stepped outside the castle and the foyer came down in a wave of rumble and dust.

I glanced around us. Half of the castle was already gone, and the other half was following. Werewolves and vampires and witches ran rampant, some fighting, some fleeing.

"We should keep moving," Thea said, her voice low. Defeated.

I nodded.

As swiftly as we could, the four of us turned to the woods and ran.

25

IT WAS LIKE DRAKE COULD READ MY MIND. WE BOTH RAN toward the cottage without even mentioning it.

But once we stepped into the clearing, my heart fell and my legs gave out.

The cottage was burned to the ground.

"No ..."

Since only Keeran and Ebby knew about the cottage, I assumed it had been Ebby. Or Morda, after Ebby had told her about this place. Or both. Or all of the Silverblood witches.

Ebby had known I had stolen the coven's heart, but I hadn't told her where I had hidden it. Nevertheless, they had retrieved it, and in the process, burnt the cottage that had been a refuge for Drake and I.

I sank to my knees as tears filled my eyes.

Drake deposited Luana down and knelt beside me. He pulled the shoulder of my ripped gown down and took a look at my wound there. "This doesn't look good."

I glanced at my shoulder. The wound had stopped

bleeding a while ago, but it still hurt. With the right healing and rest, I would be good as new, though.

I shifted my eyes to the charred wood mess in front of us. "We're in big trouble," I whispered.

Drake reached for my hand. "We'll figure it out."

"I'm glad you're confident, because I'm not." I sighed. "How can I be when Morda has the heart?"

"We'll take it back."

I rested my head on his shoulder. "Can I close my eyes and pretend this was all a dream? No, a nightmare?"

He kissed the top of my head. "You can take a few days to rest, but you know we can't pretend nothing happened."

Nothing happened ... like the heart and me. "One thing I don't understand though is how I didn't awaken the heart powers before. As far as I know, a witch queen is born, not made. I didn't suddenly become one. But why didn't it connect to me until after we met? After I stole it from the vampires?"

"I don't know." Drake inhaled deeply. "Maybe it has something to do with our bond."

"Our bond?"

"Yeah, well, I don't know, but it has to be some kind of bond. I feel a pull toward you all the freaking time. Don't you feel the same?"

"I do ..." I frowned. I hadn't given much thought to it. I thought it meant we were deeply in love, or even that we were mates, but I discarded that as vampires and werewolves only mated within their own species.

"I might be able to help with that," Luana said from behind us.

By all that was sacred, I had almost forgotten about her.

And Thomas, too. He was floating beside her. Drake had told me about him, but it was so weird seeing him like this.

"What do you mean?" I scooted closer to her and inspected her wounds. Besides all the scratches and cuts and blood, her ankle was twisted in an awkward way.

"I know someone who might know what it all means," she said.

Drake stilled. "I'm not sure. Give me one good reason we should trust you again?"

Her hazel eyes filled with tears. "Why would I lie? I followed my alpha's orders, and what do I get in return? I was abandoned by my pack and left as food offering to the crazed vampires." A tear rolled down her cheek.

"Drake, give her a break," I said, knowing he would listen to me. At least for now. "I think I can heal most of your wounds, but I'll need some ingredients first." I looked around. "I have no idea where I'll get them though."

"I know," Drake said.

I frowned at him. "What do you mean?"

"Just come with me." He picked up Luana again.

The four of us went down the hill, through a few miles into the woods, until we reached a back road. We followed the road into a small town. Drake left Luana with me at the edge of town while he stole a car.

"What?" He shrugged at me from the driver's seat. He pressed the pedal and the car lurched forward.

"You stole a car?"

"I left my silver cross pin in its place," he said, as if that made it all right. "The owner will be able to buy twenty of these now."

I shook my head, but glanced out the window.

My mind spun with so many thoughts, so many feelings. I

felt lost and broken and hopeless. I reached across the seats and grabbed Drake's hand. At least I had him with me. And this time, I wouldn't let him go.

Finally, a couple of hours later, Drake drove onto a narrow dirt road flanked by tall and thick trees. After a few minutes, the road opened into a small but neat garden. And beyond the garden, a white manor with a wraparound porch and tall windows sat at the base of the mountains.

He stopped the car in front of the house.

I frowned. "What is this?"

One corner of his lips curled up. "Our place."

"W-what?"

"I bought this place right after we got separated a few weeks ago," he said. "I thought ... I don't know. As much as I thought we would succeed, I wanted to be prepared in case we didn't. In case we had to run."

I couldn't help the smile that took over my lips. He was something else.

"I think Luana needs attention now," Thomas said from the backseat.

Luana was curled against the door, shaking and sweating.

"Right," I said, opening the car door. "Let's take her inside."

I barely had time to acknowledge the place as Drake carried Luana to one of the bedrooms on the second floor. I followed. Then he brought a box with several herbs and ingredients.

"Is this enough?" he said, putting the box down over the nightstand.

"It'll have to be."

If I had the coven's heart with me, I was sure I could heal her with magic, but since I didn't, and since I had exhausted myself fighting Morda, I required the help of salves and potions.

Thankfully, none of Luana's wounds were life threatening. The only risk was infection, but since I would take care of them, she would be fine.

She fell asleep after I treated her wounds and put her foot back into place. She was still dirty and bloodied, but she could take a bath after she rested for a while.

Thomas disappeared soon after, saying he had been holding on to his ghost form for too long. He would back later.

When it was all quiet, Drake slipped his hand in mine and guided me to the third floor.

The stairs opened to a small landing and white double doors.

"This is our bedroom," he said, pushing the doors open.

I smiled as I took the place in.

On the right, a seating area with a small couch and two armchairs in front of a cozy fireplace. On the left, a four posted king-sized bed with white gossamer over it. Everything in white wood and beige and soft yellow cushions and accents.

A happy, comfy place.

Glass doors opened to a balcony where I could see wicker chairs and table. The sun was rising, warming up the place with a golden light.

I crossed the room and pulled the thin white curtains closed. It wouldn't leave the room in total darkness, but I doubted it could hurt Drake either.

Drake sat on the bed and patted the mattress beside him. "Come here."

He didn't have to tell me twice. I practically threw myself

at him, and we both fell back on the bed, our arms around each other.

"I could stay like this forever," I mumbled, burying my face in his neck and inhaling deeply. His scent filled my nostrils and I sighed in relief.

"We could."

I pulled back. "What do you mean?"

"We can stay here. Hide from everyone else. We can pretend nothing ever happened and live our own life."

"But ... a few hours ago you were telling me we should run to fight another day. That we would get my coven's heart back later. What happened?"

"I changed my mind," he said. "I think we should hide in here forever."

"I can't. You know that. I'm the Witch Queen. You know my coven will die without me."

He sighed. "I know, I know. But do they deserve to be saved? Look at what they did to you? Morda played with you; Ebby betrayed you. They were ready to kill you."

"It's the same principle of when you wanted to go back to your coven and save the vampires from Alex's clutches. I want to take out Morda, recover the heart, and start over. I want to give my witches and our servants a better choice, a better life."

"I know." He closed his eyes. "Now even my original plan has gone down the drain. Alex is dead and only hell knows what happened to the princes and the other vampires."

I cupped his rough, handsome face. "See? We can't leave everything like that. We are better people than they are. We care about others. We have to help."

Drake locked his eyes with mine. "That's one of the reasons I love you, you know? You always want to do good."

"You too."

He wrinkled his nose. "Not always."

Of course he did; he just didn't see it. But I wouldn't argue about that now. "Besides, no matter where I hide, you know Morda will come after me now that she knows I'm the Witch Queen."

"I know." Drake groaned.

"And there's our bond too," I said. "Or whatever that is."

"Okay, okay, you can stop with our long to-do list. I know we have plenty to do." He tightened his arms around me, pressing my body to his. "For now, I want to forget it all and spend time with you."

I brushed my lips on his. "Spend time with me? How?"

He spun us around, pining me to the mattress with his body over mine. "I'll show you."

Drake leaned over me and claimed my mouth with his. His kiss wasn't soft, nor were his hands as he took off our clothes and touched me. But once he was inside me, I felt strong again. I felt like I was right where I belonged. I felt confident and sure. With him beside me, I could do anything.

We could do anything.

We would find out about our bond, we would save the vampires and the witches, and we would have a better future together. Or we would die trying.

Regardless, we would do it together. We would be together.

Forever.

***

Read the next book on Drake's and Thea's story with *The Immortal Vow* (Rite World 3: Rite of the Vampire).

THANK YOU

Thank you for reading *The Witch Queen*!

Reviews are very important for authors. If you liked my book, please consider leaving a review on your favorite vendor and/or on goodreads, please!

Grab book 3 of the series, *The Immortal Vow*, now!

Don't forget to sign up for my Newsletter to find out about new releases, cover reveals, giveaways, and more!

If you want to see exclusive teasers, help me decide on covers, read excerpts, talk about books, etc, join my reader group on Facebook: Juliana's Club!

ABOUT THE AUTHOR

While USA Today Bestselling Author Juliana Haygert dreams of being Wonder Woman, Buffy, or a blood elf shadow priest, she settles for the less exciting—but equally gratifying—life as a wife, a mother, and an author. She resides in North Carolina and spends her days writing about kick-ass heroines and the heroes who drive them crazy.

Subscribe to her mailing list to receive emails of announcement, events, and other fun stuff related to her writing and her books: www.bit.ly/JuHNL

For more information:
www.julianahaygert.com

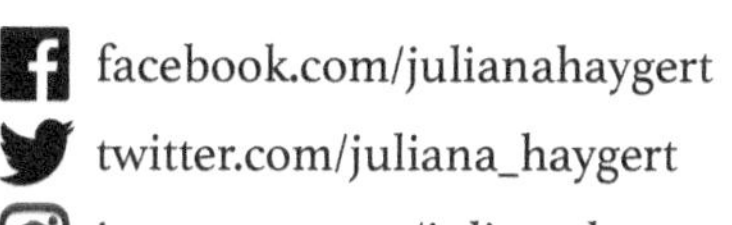

facebook.com/julianahaygert

twitter.com/juliana_haygert

instagram.com/juliana.haygert

The Blood Pact (Book 9)

The Fire Heart Chronicles

Heart Seeker (Book 1)

Flame Caster (Book 2)

Sorrow Bringer (Book 3)

Earth Shaker (Novella)

Soul Wanderer (Book 4)

Fate Summoner (Book 5)

War Maiden (Book 6)

The Everlast Series

Destiny Gift (Book 1)

Soul Oath (Book 2)

Cup of Life (Book 3)

Everlasting Circle (Book 4)

Willow Harbor Series

Hunter's Revenge (Book 3)

Siren's Song (Book 5)

Breaking Series

Breaking Free (Book 1)

Breaking Away (Book 2)

Breaking Through (Book 3)

Breaking Down (Book 4)